WHEN LOVE HITS

Morgan & Maino

KENDRA NECOLE

K. Renee Publications

Copyright © 2022 by Kendra Necole

Published By: K. Renee Publications

All rights reserved.

No part of this book may be reproduced in any form or by any electronic or mechanical means, including information storage and retrieval systems, without written permission from the author, except for the use of brief quotations in a book review.

❦ Created with Vellum

To my fiancé and love of my life, I want to thank you for showing me unconditional love and giving me a million reasons to smile. Our love was unexpected but it's truly one of a kind. You have seen me at my worst and loved me through it all. I can't wait to finally walk down the aisle and become your wife.

FRIENDLY MESSAGE

Before you begin indulging in Morgan and Maino's love story, I recommend reading my completed series, "No Looking Back." They were first introduced in that book. Thank you for the constant support. Please leave reviews.

PROLOGUE

Maurice "Maino" Pierce

Twenty Years Earlier...

Being a hustler was in my blood, and that's all I knew how to do to survive. Nonetheless, my older brother, Jason, seemed to believe I had more potential than selling grams on the block. I wasn't smart like him. He graduated at the top of his class and planned to study medicine. As for me, I barely made it through high school. My only focus was to survive without getting a bullet in my head because of the dangerous shit I did for a living.

"Lil bro, you can take the bed on the left. My roommate went home to visit his family this weekend," Jason pointed.

Jason had been attending Howard for two years and it was my first time visiting. I dropped my Nike duffle bag on his dorm room floor and glanced around the space. There were two twin-sized beds along with a desk. It wasn't anything fancy, but it was better than the drug-infested places we grew up in.

"After you get settled, I'm gonna show you around campus, and then we can go to lunch," he explained.

"Nigga, I ain't come up here for touring and nasty ass food. I'm trying to get some of this college pussy. Where are the bitches?" I rubbed my hands together with a smirk.

"Didn't I tell you that isn't how you supposed to refer to women? They are not bitches, Maurice," he scolded me.

"My bad, nigga. You right. Where the hoes at?" I nonchalantly shrugged my shoulders, and he just frowned his face.

After I took a leak, Jason showed me around the campus. I licked my lips seeing the beautiful black women. They were all different shades and body sizes. As I walked out the door, I bumped into some girl knocking her books out of her hand. I bent down to help pick them up and noticed she was undeniably a natural beauty. You definitely couldn't stare away without noticing her blemish-free, honey-brown skin, long eyelashes, downward-turned luscious lips, and tiny button nose.

"My bad, shorty. I didn't see you coming." I handed her the last book.

"Sure is your bad. You almost knocked me down with those big clown feet." She rolled her eyes.

"I said my bad. Fuck you want me to do, kill myself?" I was sarcastic.

"It won't faze me none." She pursed her lips.

"Morgan, chill out. This is my little brother," Jason jumped in to defuse the situation.

"Oh, my bad. What's up? It's nice to meet you." She smiled like she wasn't just about to curse me out.

"You sure it's good to talk to ya? A few minutes ago, you look like you were gonna kill a nigga?" I chuckled.

"That's the Baltimore girl in me. I don't play," she chuckled.

Women from B-More were feisty. They would curse you out in a minute but be cool the next, like shit didn't just get heated. All three of us headed to the library. There were black and white photos on the walls. We approached my brother's girlfriend, Eva, who was sitting at the table with books stacked up in front of her while she wrote notes. When she lifted her head, and saw me, she rolled her eyes. I met her several times, but we didn't seem to vibe. She was uppity, and I was a street nigga who didn't hold my tongue. I didn't like her for my brother.

"What's good, Eva?" I spoke to be polite after Jason shoved my arm.

"Hey." She was brief.

"Eva baby, I am about to take Maurice to get something to eat. Would you like to join us?" Jason offered with a smile.

"Baby, I actually have an exam that I need to study for, but you have fun without me." She kissed his lips.

"Oh shit. I totally forgot about the exam. Let's study together and then we can hang out," Jason was oblivious that she wasn't trying to kick it around me. "Morgan, you mind keeping my brother company until we are done studying?"

"Hell no. I ain't no babysitter." She looked me up and down as her hands were on her hips.

"I ain't no kid. I'm about to go smoke me some weed. We can link up later, big brother." I patted him on his shoulder.

"You got some weed? I have been dying to get high. My weed man just got locked up." She sighed.

"If you are looking for some fire, I got that. We just got to take a ride to my hood."

"Hell yeah, I need me an ounce." Morgan was hyped.

A panicked Eva leaped up from her seat, snatching her friend by the arm and pulling her to the side to speak in private. I knew it was about her going with me. When Morgan waved her off, walking back in my direction, I smirked. She then encircled her arm around mine, and I shot them a head nod as Jason gave me a stern look. We walked to the student parking lot, where she had a tiny little Honda. I sat in the driver's seat, and there was Nikes on the floor that looked like they belonged to a man.

"You can put those in the back." Morgan started up the engine as I tossed them in the backseat.

We drove to Trinidad, and I went to my apartment to go to my stash. I didn't know Morgan, so telling her I sold drugs was out the question. I grabbed me a pound of weed along with a couple of magnums. That night, I planned to get my dick wet. I didn't give a shit about Morgan having a man. Monogamous relationships were pointless to me. Only thing I believed is if you put two humans together, eventually they were bound to fuck. If Morgan wasn't gonna give me any pussy, I was going to fuck Tracie's hot ass. She was a chick from my neighborhood and attended the same school as them, but they probably haven't crossed paths because she was a theater major.

"What's your major?" I probed.

"I want to be an attorney. There are not enough of us to represent minorities in a system that crucifies us because of the color of our skin." She sounded passionate.

"I'm damn sure gonna need you on my payroll when I get my money right. Make sure you hit me up when you get that law degree." I smirked.

"Honey, as long as you got the money, hit me up. I'm going to take checks, money orders, credit cards, and EBT for my services."

"EBT cards? You gonna take that too?"

"Hell yeah, I don't discriminate. The only thing I ain't taking is taxes because you know IRS don't be playing fair. That shit disappears faster than a nigga who just found out he is about to become a new daddy."

"True," I agreed.

We had our weed and then went to the liquor store to get us a bottle of Hennessy before going back to Jason's dorm room. He was in a heated argument with some big ass bald dude who looked like he bench pressed people. He called himself poking Jason in the chest. I didn't know what the fuck his problem was, but he wasn't going to bitch my brother out, especially in front of his lady. With haste, I shoved the nigga back, mugging him down with my nostrils flaring. Jason immediately placed his hand on my chest, halting my steps.

"Listen, Bo. I am not gonna keep doing your homework. Enough is enough. I have carried you since high school and two years of college." Jason was fed up.

"You will do what I tell you to do, nigga. The only reason why I came to this school is because I knew you would be here to do it. Until I get drafted, you're still gonna pick up my slack or I will beat your ass." He cracked his knuckles.

Pushing Jason to the side, I cocked my fist back hitting the dude in the jaw before connecting with another fist to the side of his temple. When he was on the floor, I pulled out my gun and began repeatedly striking him with the butt of it as he grunted in pain. When Jason pulled me off the guy, his entire face was covered in blood. He damn near wasn't moving. There were looks of horror on Eva and Morgan's faces as they tightly held each other shaking.

"This isn't the hood. We are on a college campus. We don't handle arguments with physical force. Now we are all looking at jail time." Jason raked his hand down his face.

"Nigga, you are tripping. I wasn't gonna let him flex on you like some bitch."

"Maurice, violence isn't the only way to get your point across," he sighed.

"Stop calling me Maurice. He died a long time ago. My name is Maino. Listen, I love you, bro, but this college shit isn't for me. If the cops come here asking questions, y'all better keep y'all mouths closed," I threatened them.

"Bro, I will never tell on you. Just leave." Jason didn't want me around causing trouble.

I slipped my gun in the waistband of my pants and picked up my duffle bag to leave. There wasn't any point in my brother trying to save me. I was never gonna be shit but a menace to society.

Chapter One
MAURICE "MAINO" PIERCE

Present...

I despised a thief, and anybody who took from my children's mouths had to pay the ultimate price with their lives. Tightly holding the handle of a meat cleaver, I approached my accountant, Micha, as he silently sobbed. He was tied up in duct tape to a rolling chair. With the tip of my blade, I lifted his chin to look me in the eyes, and he flinched in discomfort. It was so sharp I made him bleed a little bit.

"Did you really think you were gonna steal from me and I wouldn't notice? You think I'm some dumb nigga?" I spoke through my gritted teeth.

For six months, Micha had been putting fifty thousand dollars of my money into an overseas account that I didn't authorize. My lawyer discovered it after he started keeping a second book for my many businesses. He brought it to my attention and I immediately took action.

"No, Mr. Pierce. I don't look at you that way, sir." He shook his head with tears on his cheeks.

"Good," I spoke calmly and cut the tape from his body, "Now put your hands on the table."

"What?"

"Put your hands on the fuckin' table!" I yelled.

A sheen of sweat rolled off his forehead as he hesitantly placed them on the table. Without warning, I swung the blade and penetrated through his flesh and bone, cutting off his right hand. Blood started spewing everywhere. He was yelling in agony and biting down on his quivering lip. I quickly removed my Glock 19 from my waist, sending two shots to his dome. His head dropped immediately on the table like a puppet. I smirked before picking up the Cristal bottle and poured me some aged scotch. There was nothing like having a good drink after putting in some work. I had my cleaning crew collect his body. Then, they put him in my underground morgue.

My office was spotless, as if nothing had taken place there. After I left the funeral home, I headed to DCA airport. I had to catch a flight to Milan for a good friend of mine, who was celebrating their seventy-fifth birthday. His name was Giovanni Bianchi. When I first began making a name for myself on the streets, he would help me clean my money through his trucking company. It wasn't common for African Americans and Italians to associate, especially regarding business. Nonetheless, he took to me like family. We met through his nephew, Rafael, who was my attorney. Even though Mr. Bianchi and I didn't see each other often because he had moved back to Milan after he retired, it was still love.

When I arrived at the airport, I got my ticket and checked my black Gucci duffel bag in before waiting to board the plane. Despite all the money I made in the streets, I was a simple man. I didn't get on private planes or jets unless my kids were traveling with me. Otherwise, I always flew first-class and purchased both seats so no one would sit by me. I enjoyed having my space. I hated being crunched up. Sometimes, I couldn't do that, though.

I showed my ticket when it was time to board the plane, and the woman scanned it with a smile. I plopped down on the leather seat and slipped on my Beats to tune out everything. That's when Morgan Reid, unexpectedly strolled down the narrow aisle wearing a pink bonnet with her Louis Vuitton purse hiked on her shoulder, looking like she had an attitude. We immediately locked eyes, but neither one of us spoke. She began looking down at her ticket for her seat number. I could've sworn the blood drained from her face. She marched up to the stewardess and showed her ticket. I watched Morgan release a sigh before approaching me.

"Excuse me, sir. That's my seat by the window," Morgan acted like she didn't know me and frowned her face.

Morgan disliked me ever since I pistol-whipped that football player and almost got her, Eva, and Jason expelled from school. They refused to testify on me, so I never faced any jail time. As far as the dude, he was so terrified I would come back to finish the job, he lied to the campus police that it was some hazing gone wrong and ended up transferring. Occasionally, when I did go around to see my brother, after he married Eva, Morgan still kept her distance. They both couldn't stand me.

While Morgan was sliding past to get to the window, she accidentally rubbed her ass against my dick and then dropped down on the seat, huffing. Before placing her purse on the floor, she grabbed her neck pillow. She then knocked my arm off the armrest and began looking at her phone. I just shook my head chuckling, putting on my seatbelt. We were instructed to turn our devices on airplane mode. During takeoff, Morgan unexpectedly gripped my arm and sank her nails into my skin.

"Don't tell me you're scared of flying," I chuckled.

"No, I just don't like the takeoff part. My stomach always drops," she explained and slipped her AirPods in her ears.

For the first couple of hours on the flight, Morgan and I didn't even speak. When the stewardess pushed her cart down the aisle, she stopped in front of our seats, showing a bottle of 2008 Dom Pérignon.

"Sir, do you and your wife want anything to drink? If you don't want Dom Pérignon, we also have Chandon." She smiled politely.

"Sorry, lady, I am not his wife. He could only wish to be that lucky. He isn't my type," Morgan was blunt. "I'll take me a glass of Chandon, and keep them coming. I paid a lot of money for this seat. Damn sure gonna get my money's worth."

The woman slightly chuckled, amused at Morgan's antics before focusing her attention on me, "And for you, sir?"

"The same," I replied as the stewardess nodded her head.

Within two minutes, Morgan gulped down her champagne from the crystal flute glass like she was drinking malt liquor. I couldn't help but laugh when she discreetly slipped out two small mini-Vodka's from her purse. She began looking around before pouring them into her glass.

"You're gonna sit right next to me getting fucked up and not share?" I raised my eyebrow.

"You didn't put in on this, man. Now, mind your business." She sipped.

"For real? This champagne ain't doing anything for me."

"Fine, but you better not rat me out." She discreetly handed me a tiny vodka.

After drinking two mini vodkas, I laid my head back to rest my eyes. Suddenly, my stomach started growling like a mothafucka. The stewardesses finally came around and started serving a slight dinner. Creamy tomato soup, salad, and pan-fried sea bass with mashed potatoes was what they were serving. That little bit of food didn't even get me full. It damn sure wasn't seasoned the way I preferred. I wanted some soul food.

"That food was horrible. I'm glad I packed me something to eat. For all that, I could've stayed in coach and got crackers," she complained.

When Morgan took out some fried chicken from her bag, my mouth began watering. I intently watched her rip the crispy skin off the bone and swallowed without dropping any crumbs. She sat right in my face eating away without offering.

"What are you looking at, Maino? You ain't never see a woman eat chicken before? All in my grill," she got sassy.

"You ain't gonna share?" I licked my lips.

"Oh, hell no. I already used one of my nice cards today. You got some liquor from me, don't push it. This chicken is all mine." She licked her fingers.

"Greedy ass," I mumbled.

"Hungry ass," she winked.

"Why are you going to Milan? Vacation or work?" I made slight conversation.

"My birthday. I'm turning forty and fabulous."

"Is Eva joining you?" I probed.

Eva was my ex-sister-in-law. She was married to my brother for years and we never got along. She always acted like she was better than me because she was some big shot professor and I sold drugs. After she caught my brother cheating, they got a divorce. Once they were no longer together, I thought I would never have to deal with her uppity ass again, but you know what they say. Never say never. She began dating my son, Ace. People probably thought she was keeping it in the family but that wasn't the case. Neither Ace or Eva knew I was his father, until they were seriously dating. I wasn't able to raise Ace because his mother Tracie kept him away from me, and had another man pretending to be his real pops. When the truth was revealed, Ace and I started to build a relationship, leaving me no choice but to deal with Eva.

"Nope, it's just me. We plan to do something for my birthday when I return. Why? You want to buy me a gift?"

"What do you want for a gift? I got you." I was willing to get her something as her eyes widened with surprise.

"Four stacks so I can buy a man with a big penis," she laughed.

"You ain't got to buy that. Shit, I got one of those." I shot her a grin.

"Eww. Nobody wants to think about your penis." She frowned her face.

Our flight landed around six at night. We went our separate ways, getting into our limos that were waiting for us at the airport. I was staying at Bulgari Hotel Milano. As I stepped on the elevator, I went to press the button for the top floor, and Morgan barged in with her rolling bag.

"Oh, hell. Nigga, you're following me?" she looked me up and down with her lips scrunched up.

"I was just getting ready to ask you the same thing." I wasn't trying to look like a creep.

"You must be a fool because Morgan Reid don't want you, so I damn sure wouldn't follow you. Hit floor number seven."

"Can you say please?"

"Nope." She pursed her lips.

The elevator arrived on Morgan's floor and she left with her phat ass bouncing.

As she was switching down the hallway, I quickly stuck my head out and shouted, "Happy Birthday, old bird!"

"Kiss my ass!" she yelled back.

I headed downstairs after settling in my hotel room and went to a restaurant to get me something to eat. The host escorted me to a table before handing me a menu. I glanced around taking in the environment and noticed Morgan sitting on the patio sipping on a glass of wine while eating a T-bone steak. I stood up from my seat and made my way to her table. I figured she wouldn't mind my company.

"My bad. I'm late," I played it cool.

"Excuse me, negro? Why are you here? I didn't invite you to eat with me. Now, leave. I'm trying to enjoy my meal."

"I know, but I thought you could enjoy some company. You're here alone and I am too. We might as well eat together."

"I'm here alone by choice, but you're probably here without a woman because you're an asshole," she laughed.

"I couldn't agree with you more. Now, can I join you or not, because I am starving?"

"Fine, but don't talk too much. I like to eat in peace and quiet."

Although Morgan made it clear she wasn't fond of me, I felt bad she was spending time alone for her birthday. We hung out for about an hour before I left and sent another bottle of champagne up to her room, along with a chocolate cake for her to celebrate.

Chapter Two
MORGAN REID

A diva only turned forty once, so I had to treat myself and not cheat myself. For my birthday, I booked a trip to Milan. The architecture of the buildings was beautiful, and there were so many fashion places to shop. However, there wasn't anything better than celebrating with my girls. When I returned from vacation, they took me out to dinner at one of my favorite Brazilian steak houses, Fogo De Chao. I smiled, watching the waitress present me with a Louis Vuitton handbag cake. As we cut the cake, Eva said a few heartfelt words. I used my napkins to dab the tears off my cheek. When the two of us met at our freshman seminar in college, we instantly connected. I was free-spirited with a wicked tongue, and she was a goodie two shoes, who wouldn't dare do anything wrong. Still, we became more than best friends. She became my sister.

During the darkest times of my life, she stayed by my side unconditionally without any judgment. She taught me how to act like a lady and to use my articulation to settle disputes rather than through physical violence. I was still learning restraint because I would smack a bitch quick for disrespecting me.

"Hoe, you got me crying. I'm a thug," I wiped my tears.

"I love you, boo. Always be you because you're the life of the party." Eva kissed my cheek.

"What y'all trying to get in to now? I'm trying to party." Shanice was excited.

"I want to do some bald-head hoe shit. My parents got the kids," Lovely slurred.

"Let's go see some big dick strippers." I was hyped and tossed my drink back.

"Strippers? I never been to the strip club. I don't want to see any half-naked men when I am about to become a married woman." Eva frowned.

"Oh, be quiet, Ms. Poppins. Won't you live a little? If you don't like it, we can go see the women. I want to party," I said to Eva and she sighed.

We finished dinner and climbed in a party bus that drove us to the gentlemen's club. The music was popping as we found a table in front of the stage waiting for the show. A male dancer with ebony skin and long dreads strutted out wearing a police uniform. He snatched off his shirt, exposing his glistening body, and began rubbing his fingers down his abs while licking his lips.

"What are you waiting for? Let me see the dick. Take it off," I yelled and stuck out my tongue.

"Go head, baby. You look like you got sausage for days!" Shanice yelled while holding her drink.

"Drop them draws, chocolate thunder." Lovely shimmied in her seat.

"Keep it on, please." Eva looked disgusted.

When the fine ass stripper finally snatched his pants off, showing his dick, it was huge. All the women began tossing money on stage as he gyrated his hips. Poor Eva looked like she wanted to pass out from stress. She was such a goodie two shoes, but I loved her to death. The stripper wanted to bring someone on stage and strutted towards our table with his dick swinging. He looked at us with sensual glances but extended his hands to me. I tossed back my drink, took off his police hat and put it on my head, and gripped hold of his arm. With a devious smirk, he lifted me on the stage floor. Then, he sensually began grinding his body as I wrapped my legs around his waist, enjoying the dance.

After several drinks, we staggered back to our party bus and went to see the female dancers. It was my first time attending, so I didn't know what to expect. I told my girls they could invite their husbands. All of us were tossing money on the strippers acting a fool while laughing, when the fellas came in, hyped. I swung my neck seeing Maino stroll in behind them wearing all black while smoking a cigar. I didn't invite that sucka to come party with us. As I sipped on my fruity drink, a stripper with pecan-colored skin and a bodacious body came to give me a lap dance. She began making her ass clap in front of me as I tossed money. Maino poured champagne on her booty. I could tell from the way he bobbed his head, that he was in his element. The strippers in our section were very familiar with him and was breaking their necks to get his attention.

"Get nasty, girl and arch that back in her face," Maino instructed the stripper that was dancing in front of me.

"Just like that, baby. Work for that money, honey." I tossed another bill.

"Pop that pussy. Harder, baby. Tell her pop that shit harder, Morgan," Maino looked at me with his hooded eyes.

"You heard that man. Pop it harder and I need to hear those cheeks smacking." I was feeding off of Maino's energy.

I couldn't stand Maino, but he had a point. She was gonna have to work for my money. When my favorite song, "WAP," blared through the speakers, I joined the strippers and began twerking with them. Maino kept his eyes glued to my body as I slowly moved to the beat. I didn't care if that nigga looked because he would never put his dirty hands on me.

"Stop staring, fool. This dance ain't free. Toss those stacks," I told Maino.

He tossed that money so quickly.

"Go lower for a nigga," he slurred his words, "I like to see the pussy pop."

"Pussy pop. Nobody can pop it better than me. Show me the cash, and you can see this juicy chocolate ass. I bet that's what you want to see. Right, big Maino?"

"Yeah, I do," he was mesmerized.

I was faded out my mind and jumped down into a split on the floor, shaking my ass, giving Maino and everybody else a show. Eva's eyes grew ten times their size as she leaped up from the leather couch like somebody's mommy and snatched me up, escorting me out the strip club. All I remembered was her tucking me in bed and kissing my cheek before she turned off the lights in my room.

The next morning, the beaming sun peering through my bedroom woke me up like an alarm clock. The side of my head was throbbing, and I could barely open my eyes. My cat, Tink, was loudly meowing, so I figured my baby boy needed to be fed. He rushed to his bowl the moment I poured him some food. Then, I went to the kitchen to make some tea to ease my hangover. As I placed the tea kettle filled with water on the stove, my cellphone started ringing. I raked my hands down my face letting out a sigh before placing the phone on speaker.

"Hey, Grandma Frances." I rolled my eyes.

"Damn, shame. I raised you, and you won't even pick up my call? How long has it been this time?" she spoke in a shaky voice from her old age.

"Not long enough," I mumbled under my breath, "How have you been? Are taking your medication for your diabetes? You need to stay healthy."

"I'm fine. It's not like you care. I took you in when nobody wanted you because you were a bastard child. This is what I get? Your ass to kiss? No matter what your job is, you still a heathen sinner who is going to hell. I can't stand the woman you have become. You're loud, ghetto, and stupid, just like your mama." She ended the call.

Gritting my teeth, I slammed my phone, shattering the screen. She always knew how to get me worked up, and I hated when I allowed her to make me feel weak. She took me in when I was a little girl because her crackhead daughter couldn't get her shit right. Pastor Frances

Emma Reid, damn sure won't let me forget it. She treated the congregation like gold, but ruled her household with an iron fist. I couldn't stand that old ass woman. Honestly, I wished she would've let me go to foster care.

Chapter Three
MAURICE "MAINO" PIERCE

I was rocking back and forth in a corner in my living room with tears rolling down my face because mama had burned a cigarette on Jason's back. He squinted his eyes in pain and let out an uncontrollable cry. After that, he became silent and took his punishment. When mama was done with him, she placed the butt in her mouth, took a drag, and approached me.

My first instinct was to hop off the floor, bolt towards the front door and escape. She must've read my mind because I didn't act fast enough before that crazy woman gripped the collar of my shirt and flung me around like a puppet. As she hovered over top of me with a menacing glare, I closed my eyes. I wasn't going to put up a fight. She repeatedly trailed my back with the burning tip of her cigarette butt, sending intense pains throughout my body. It was so intense that I almost passed out. At the same time, I realized how tough Jason was for taking that pain.

The sound of someone ringing my doorbell woke me from my sleep. Standing up from the couch, I opened the door and saw my son, Ace, holding a black garment bag. We were supposed to meet at noon at the tux shop, and I overslept. Ace handed me my tux and I let him in my house. He sat down on the couch and began checking his phone. Raking my hands down my face, I released a heavy sigh. On the most important days of his life, with him planning to get married, I was still fucking up as a father. I felt like a piece of shit. My relationship with Ace was still a work in progress. The two of us often spent time together going to different places in the DMV.

"Ace, I'm sorry, man. I overslept and didn't hear my alarm." I was annoyed at myself.

"You good, Maino. You overslept. Shit happens." He shrugged his shoulders without being upset.

"I know, but when it comes to my kids, I don't want this shit to happen. I am gonna make sure not to miss anything else." I was adamant.

"I appreciate that, man. Since you weren't able to see me in my suit, I took pictures. I hope that ain't corny." Ace was funny a dude.

"Not all, man. Let me see them." I didn't mind looking at the pictures.

He proudly swiped through the pictures. It made me feel good knowing that he wanted to share his meaningful moments with me.

"You trying to get something to eat?" I wanted to make it up to him.

"Yeah, why not?" he agreed.

I went to jump in the shower, and we headed out to breakfast. I took him to Ted's Bulletin in Eastern Market. As I was looking down at the menu to see what I wanted to eat, I had got a call from my right-hand man, Rich. He was telling me to get to the funeral home. I couldn't catch a break to be a father to my child. I tried, and just like that, I had to tend to business and leave.

"I have an emergency I have to tend to at the funeral home." I felt like a shitty father.

Ace didn't seem to trip, but I hated to leave him like that. After dapping him up, I made haste out of the restaurant and jumped in my car, zooming down the street. When I pulled up to the spot, Tracie was there holding a sign calling me a deadbeat drug dealer, making a scene for the people who were walking past. With my jaws locked, I approached her, and she jumped back screaming like I was getting ready to put my hands on her. I snatched the sign from her hands and towered over her as she tripped onto the ground. She pulled her lips into a vindictive ass smirk.

"Why the fuck you making trouble, Tracie? You just made me leave Ace alone for breakfast. I was trying to bond with our son and you doing this stupid shit!" I spoke through my gritted teeth.

"If I don't stop, what you're gonna do? Hit me?" she was provoking me. "I can't believe my son wants a relationship with you and not me. I dedicated my life to him and gave him everything." She was angry.

It wasn't my fault Ace wanted a relationship with me. She kept him from me. I never left. I was kept outside the gate. She had a gambling problem and was a manipulative liar. When he found out I was his biological father, it just put the nail in the coffin for everything.

"You're the one who lied to him all these years! Not me!" I didn't have time for her shit.

"I don't regret my decision. You ain't shit, Maurice. I hope my son sees you for what type of monster you really are, you son of a bitch." She was full of resentment.

Like the nasty bitch she was, Tracie hawked spit in my face before speed walking towards her car. As the glob rolled down my face, I had to suppress everything in me to not react. No, I didn't put my hands on women but getting spat on was grounds for getting yo' ass murked. She was lucky that Ace loved her enough, even luckier that he wanted to get to know me. Building a relationship with my son was more important than putting a bullet in her head.

* * *

My skin was caked in paint as I took cover behind a big ass tree holding two balloons filled with paint. We were having a men against women balloon fight for Eva and Ace's co-ed sports-themed Bachelor/Bachelorette party. I was having a good ol' time fucking shit up, until Morgan walked up to me with a devious smirk and smashed a balloon over my head. As the paint rolled down my face, her crazy ass started twerking like caramel kitten.

"That's game, mothafucka. We some bad bitches." Morgan was hyped for nothing.

"Y'all won by one lil' ass point." I was being a sore loser.

"Stop hating. Nobody didn't tell your big goofy ass to hide behind that tree like nobody couldn't see you," Morgan laughed.

"Yea, just like nobody didn't tell you to wear that Harriet Tubman headscarf around your head," I clapped back.

The fellas knew what I was talking about. They were laughing like shit. Morgan tossed her water bottle at me, but I dodged it. She was fired up that I got under her skin and I enjoyed it. Her reactions made me feel like I had control. All she kept doing was mumbling under her breath and cutting her eyes at me. She wanted to kick my ass. Shrugging my shoulders nonchalantly with a smirk, I grabbed my towel from my gym bag and wiped some of the paint off my face.

"Aight, so the next game we gonna do is a team relay race. I already picked the teams," Easton announced.

Easton pulled out some custom-made jerseys in different colors representing the teams and began handing them to everyone. My eyebrows slammed together when I noticed Morgan holding the same color as me. She was probably going to make us lose on purpose. I looked at Ace, and he just shook his head, laughing like he could read my mind.

"Why do I have to be on this nigga team?" Morgan pointed at me with her top lip curved as I slipped on my jersey that had my name on the back.

Her friend Eva couldn't stand me either. It had been like that for years.

"You ain't got a man, so you're stuck with me. This is the closest you're going to get to a relationship." I smirked.

"Negro, yes I do got a man. His name is big black. Mind your business." She rolled her neck and put her hand in my face.

"Stop all that talkin' and put your shirt on. We need to come out on top for this race." I was worried about winning.

Morgan couldn't stand me. She was huffing when I was tying our legs together with a scarf. We approached the long rope that was supposed to be the starting line. When Rachel tossed a blue bandana in the air, signaling us to go, I wrapped my arm around Morgan's waist, but she pushed me off with a scowl on her face.

"Don't put your greasy hands on me." She got feisty.

"It ain't even like that. I'm trying to win. We already behind, c'mon." I shook my head.

Trying to talk to Morgan was like talking to a brick wall. She swore I was trying to feel her up. Her impatient ass kept trying to pull me instead of letting me do the work. I was the one with the muscle. We at least had to make an effort and Morgan was falling every chance she got. We were looking like some bums, and I couldn't take that shit anymore. I wrapped my arms around her body, picked her up, and manhandled her ass towards the finish line. Just when we thought we had a chance to win, somebody's damn ball rolled in our path and tripped us up. Morgan and I ended up falling on top of each other, with me landing on top of her ass.

"All because of you, we lost, and top of that you trying to feel on my ass." Morgan swore I was trying to cop a feel.

It was cool doing different things and taking part in the events of Ace's life. Glad I could feel somewhat like a father for once because being a killer and a drug dealer was all I knew for the longest time. I was going to make sure to give Ace nothing but the best. After all the games, I rented out a dining spot at a private estate for the whole family and hired a private chef to cook the food. We were sitting in a room with diamond-studded chandeliers hanging above us, with an open window view of the Potomac River waiting to be served an elegant feast. A lot of distinctive chatter and side conversations were going on. Everyone was having a great time. I hired waiters and waitresses too. One of them handed me a bottle of Ace of Spades and popped open the cork as some of the champagne fizzed down on the floor.

"Eva, I am so happy for you, girl. You deserve nothing but happiness, and I'm so glad you found your soulmate. Ace, you're a man, and a great father. I'm so happy my bestie found you. I still can't believe that nigga is your father, though, but y'all don't act nothing alike. Wow... God does work miracles." Morgan was being loud as hell and she was tipsy as hell.

"You could get a good man too if you change your attitude," I stood up from my chair and projected my voice.

"I don't need to change anything about me, baby," she was

offended. "The reason I'm single is by choice. I can have any man I want eating out the palm of my hand, including you, if I was desperate. Now stop worrying about who I'm giving my attention to and focus on your basic hoes." Morgan pursed her lips.

For her not to like me so much, she sure wanted to get my attention a lot. I sarcastically clapped my hands as she continued to drink her champagne. She swore she was a queen. If I really spat game at Morgan, I would have her dropping her panties and climbing on my dick like a cheetah climbing up a tree.

Chapter Four
MORGAN REID

My head was throbbing, cradling my God baby, Ava, in my arms, trying to soothe her from crying. She had been screaming from the top of her lungs for over an hour, and I felt so damn overwhelmed. At first, I was super excited about keeping her for the weekend so her parents could celebrate their honeymoon at some bed and breakfast in Virginia.

"Oh, my goodness. Please stop crying, baby. You're killing me," I sighed.

The doorbell rang, so I placed her in her portable crib, and went to answer the door. It was Maino standing on the other side holding a duffle bag. I curved my head to the side looking him up and down.

"How do you know where the hell I live?" I was annoyed.

"Ace must've not told you. He gave me your address and thought you could use a hand. From the way my granddaughter is crying, I'm glad he did. Let me in." He thought he could just step foot in my condo.

"No, fool. I don't know you like that. This is my place. Ace ain't running nothin' up in here." I stopped him with my hands on his chest.

"And that little girl is a part of me. Look, Morgan, I ain't trying to argue. How long she's been crying?" he was concerned.

"For like an hour and she won't stop. It's driving me up the got damn wall," I sighed.

"Then, let me help you," he suggested.

He must've read my mind because I damn sure needed some help. I guess hating him put me at a disadvantage and had me putting my pride to the side. I allowed Maino in. He dropped his duffle bag on the floor before going to wash his hands. The moment he scooped Ava in his arms and rocked her while softly singing to her, she calmed down. I was shocked.

"Did you give her a bottle?" he probed.

"I did, but she won't latch on." I was frustrated.

"Eva probably breast feeds her, so she prefers that. You got to be patient with the bottle. Go warm it up please and I will feed her," he instructed me.

I couldn't stand his ass telling me what to do in my own home.

I rolled my eyes at Mr. Know It All and went to warm up the bottle. He got all comfortable on my couch laying Ava on top of his chest, softly rubbing her back. She even smiled at him. Ain't that a bitch! She cried on my ass. After handing him the bottle, he cradled her in his arms before placing it gently in her mouth. I intently watched her suck the nipple. Occasionally, she got fussy, but she drank every drop. Maino gently patted her back and made her burp. After feeding her, he put her in the crib for a nap. He shot me a wink and sat back on my couch with his feet up. The nerve of him, but not in my house. I marched over there and slapped his feet down. He just shook his head, chucking.

"Don't be putting your damn feet on my table. Thank you for helping with Ava. Now you can go." I pointed to the door.

"I ain't leaving my grandbaby with you. Where am I sleeping?" he probed.

I looked over at his duffle bag and rolled my eyes. There was no way I was letting a man who didn't belong to me be in my personal space.

"Excuse me? You're not staying here. I already know you kill, so that means you steal too." I was blunt.

"It's only for the weekend and I will stay out the way. I think we both know you need me." He smirked.

I hated to admit it, but he had a point. Being with Ava alone was driving me insane. All I could do was sigh and drop my shoulders in defeat as he sat there on my couch with a proud look on his face. I know what he was thinking. He thought he had won. Damn... I guess he did. At that point, he had me wanting to rather fuck with a small dick nigga for the rest of my life than need Maino's help.

"Fine, you can sleep on the couch. Don't be eating up all my groceries." I was so annoyed.

"Don't worry. You done forgot, I can buy the whole a grocery store and the people in it," he reminded me of his position.

On the bright side, Ava was sleep, and I made it clear to Maino that he was to stay his ass on the couch. Dealing with those two called for a well-deserved bubble bath. I was sipping on my glass of wine with bubbles soaking and exfoliating my skin. I didn't get out until I finished the whole bottle. I was tipsy as hell climbing out of the tub, not to mention naked, but I had remembered that I had an uninvited guest. I surely rushed to close my bedroom door and quickly got dressed. Of course, I had to check on Maino to make sure he wasn't putting shit in his pocket, and I had my cat, Tinkerbell, with me to sniff anything else I couldn't. To my surprise, it didn't even look like he moved a muscle. He was lounging on the couch watching sports like he paid the bills. His eyes widened when I placed Tinkerbell on the floor. He leaped up from the couch like a rat ran past him. From his body language, I could've sworn he was afraid of cats.

"Oh no. Don't tell me big bad Maino is afraid of little pussy cats," I laughed.

"I ain't scared. I just don't like those sneaky mothafuckas. Don't you got a cage to put him in until I bounce?" he tried to tell me what to do, and I wasn't having it.

"Nigga, please. This is Tink and my place. He ain't going nowhere. Right, baby?" I kissed my cat who was purring.

"You kissing all rat right now. You know how many mice he probably ate." He looked disgusted.

"Probably the same as many dicks I ate." I winked.

I grabbed a banana and deep throated it as he looked at me with gigantic eyes. After two big bites, I tossed the peel in the trash, went back to my bedroom, and left him on baby duty. He was there to help me anyway.

Later on that afternoon ...

"Come feed her," Maino tried to hand me a bottle, and I frowned.

"Nope, she doesn't like when I give her the bottle." My feelings were hurt.

Ava only wanted her grandfather to feed her, change her diaper, and play with her on the floor. I felt left out in my own damn place.

"It's not that she doesn't like you. She knows you're nervous. You need to relax when you are caring for her. Come here, let me help you."

I dragged my feet on the carpet and sat down on the couch next to him. When he placed Ava in my arms, she began fussing. He instructed me to rock her slowly, while talking to her. Surprisingly, it worked. Then, I tried to give her the bottle. He placed his gigantic hands-on top of mine to hold it steady.

All the fussiness and crying that Ava was doing was probably because she needed to get some fresh air. The weather felt great, so we put Ava in the stroller and took her outside to a park that was next to my building. As I pushed her, Maino walked next to us on guard like we were precious cargo. Yes, we were. At the park, we sat down on a wooden bench while Ava was still sleeping. She was so pretty with her honey-brown colored skin, long eyelashes, and heart-shaped lips.

"You don't want any children?" Maino probed.

"Hell no! I'm a career-driven woman. I ain't got time for kids, only for the ones who are not mine, like my Ava. Come here, baby." I gently pinched her baby cheeks.

"Damn. Why you say it like that? I think you would be a good mother." I think Maino was just trying to butter me up.

For as long as I could remember, I never desired to have children. Shit, even as a child, I didn't want to have a baby doll. Growing up with a mother for a crackhead, only taught me about survival, and that's all I ever knew how to do.

"You're really good with babies. How many kids do you have other than Ace?" I probed.

A street nigga like him probably had a lot of kids, plus baby mama drama. He looked like the type who spread his semen around town with his nasty ass. His face lit up with joy, and a gigantic smile appeared on his lips.

"I have two girls and they are my world. As far as Ace, it's good to have him in my life," he was so honest.

As Maino and I were talking about his children, I spotted my ex, Pernell, walking his dog. We dated for about two months, but after catching him going through my underwear drawer, I deleted his number. When he approached me smirking, I rolled my eyes. Just looking at him made me feel dirty.

"Morgan, I thought that was you. How you been, girl?" he smiled.

"I have been great. Just had a baby and got married to the love of my life," I lied while wrapping my arms around Maino's shoulders.

I was in a real tight spot, so I had to sell it by climbing on Maino's lap. I could've sworn his dick got hard under my ass, and it wasn't a bad experience either. I could tell that thang was big.

"Oh wow. I thought you didn't want a family?" Pernell looked dumbfounded.

"I didn't, but I found the one who changed all that for me. Right, honey?" I gave Maino a look to play along.

"Yeah, all this belong to me, homie," Maino played along.

Maino took full advantage of the situation, cupped the side of my face, and dipped his tongue in my mouth like a strawberry. Out of all the things he could have done to play along, I had no clue why that mothafucka was kissing me, but I wasn't complaining. We had to make it look real so that creep could go away. Pernell didn't want anything to do with me after he saw that. After he walked off, Maino pulled back from my lips while my breathing was still elevated. A part of me thought it was interesting, but I didn't want to show any interest, so I smacked Maino across his face and told him not to put his damn lips on me ever again. I stood up from his lap and sat back on the bench. It was going to be a long ass weekend.

Chapter Five
MAURICE "MAINO" PIERCE

The side of my face stung like shit after Morgan's feisty ass smacked me for giving her a kiss. I was only trying to get under her skin and got what I deserved, but her lips did feel good against mine. It would have been worth getting smacked again. I could tell from the way she was squirming on the bench looking at her phone, her panties were drenched. If she wanted me to put her legs over her head and serve her some dick, a nigga was down to fuck.

"You do know it's a crime putting your lips on people without their consent? Don't touch me again or I'm putting your black ass in jail." She rolled her eyes.

"You ain't gonna do shit but sit here and enjoy this good ass weather. Who was that nigga anyway?" I probed and rubbed the bottom of my chin.

She snaked her neck and rolled her eyes, "If you must know, nosey, he is my ex-boyfriend."

"That nigga doesn't even look like your type. You probably was only with him for the money," I accused.

"Money don't make me dance. If it did, I would be riding your dick right now. Ain't you rich?" she pursed her lips.

"I got more money than you can spend and too much dick for you to handle." I licked my lips and her eyes widened.

"Nigga, please. Your dick is probably smaller than them Vienna sausages that come in the can. Nobody wants to see that. No thanks," she laughed.

"You wanna find out?" I smirked, ready to unzip my pants zipper.

"Never will I ever want to see anything between your legs. I already know it's been in all types of basic bitches." She seemed jealous.

When my grandbaby Ava started fussing in her stroller, I stood to pick her up. She immediately relaxed in my arms, looking at me with a little smirk. I wasn't able to be a part of her father's life because of his vindictive ass mother, but I damn sure was going to be present in hers without a doubt. We stayed at the park until Ava shitted up her back, ruining her clothes. She even put it on my pants, so I smelled like shit. Morgan thought it was hilarious. I didn't want to put Ava in her stroller because she would get it dirty, so my only choice was to hold her.

The entire walk back to her condo, she kept calling us Shitty McGee. It was all good though, because she wouldn't be laughing when she found out she was going to be the one doing the changing. When we finally arrived at the condo, Morgan opened the front door pushing the stroller in as I followed behind her, cradling a sleeping Ava. She didn't seem to care she was shitty, but I frowned my face because her stench was engrossing my nostrils.

"Baby girl, you stink something terrible. You got to get a bath." I smiled at Ava, who was still sleeping.

"Make sure you don't put that shit on my new carpet. I just got it steamed." Morgan smirked.

With my eyebrows slammed together, I watched Morgan plop down on the couch and pick up the remote control to turn on the television, not lifting a finger to help. I had something for her ass. While she was laughing at some show, I gently laid Ava on her leather couch before picking up my duffel bag to go take a shower.

"I got to get cleaned up. Handle that diaper," I told Morgan and she looked like she was getting ready to snap.

"You fucker. I know you didn't lay her down on my new couch. Oh, you're going to be cutting me a check if it's ruined." She gritted her teeth.

I pulled out two rolls of cash from my pants pocket and placed them on her glass table with a smirk. She looked at it before picking up Ava and began stomping off, bumping me to the side. She was dramatic, but I liked it. I went to the bathroom and dropped my duffle bag onto the floor. Then, I stripped out my clothes, getting naked. My tattoos hid the scars from my troubled childhood. Covering them helped a little, but I was still messed up mentally. As I stood under the showerhead, the water ran down my face, and I closed my eyes, taking a deep breath.

When I heard snickering and the door shutting, I knew Morgan was up to no good. The sounds of meowing immediately caught my attention, so I quickly pulled the shower curtain back. There was her ginger-colored cat licking his paws. The hairs on my body rose up as my eyes widened like two saucers. For as long as I could remember, I didn't like cats. I was attacked by an old gray one back in the day.

"Aye, Morgan! Stop playing, girl, and come get this damn cat. I ain't playing with you!" I yelled.

"Big bad, Maino. How about you pick Tink up? He isn't going to bite," she laughed.

"Let this little nigga come close to me and I'm gonna boot that mothafucka," I threatened.

"Touch my Tink and it's your ass. I don't play about him. He's the only loyal nigga I got, and I will go to war behind my baby. Now apologize for kissing me earlier or I ain't coming to get him."

"Damn, you win. I'm sorry for you enjoying that kiss."

"I didn't enjoy that shit. Your lips are crusty, and your beard smells like the tip of someone's ass crack." She was bluffing.

"You're a damn lie. That's the best kiss you ever received in your life." I was confident.

"Since you're so adamant it was, make sure you give the same kiss to Tink," she laughed loudly.

"For real, Morgan? Come get this cat. He is starting to act crazy." I watched Tink roll on the floor, biting into his fur like he had some flees or some shit.

"Not until you apologize." I could hear the humor in her voice.

"I'm sorry for kissing you and leaving you with the shitty diaper. Damn, are you happy now? Come get this cat so I can finish taking a shower. The water is starting to get cold," I ranted.

A smirk was on Morgan's face as she entered the bathroom and picked up her furball, cuddling him to her chest. When she snuggled his nose against hers, I grimaced. She was just nasty and weird. There was no way in hell I would be getting that close to a smelly ass cat. I bet the niggas she was dealing with were cat lovers too. She got ready to shut the door, and I pulled open the curtain to show my dick. With a smirk on my face, I began jerking it as her eyes widened. For a moment, she got lost in lust, but eventually snapped out of it and closed the door with a scowl. I shook my head, laughing, and continued to take a shower.

After I was done getting fresh, I slipped on a tank top and some basketball shorts. Then, I went to the living room to chill. Morgan had my granddaughter cuddled in her arm carefully feeding her a bottle while that nigga Tink sat protectively at her bare feet. Bitch ass nigga. I ordered some food for us and we ate in silence. When Morgan received a phone call, she took it in the back for some privacy. As I laid a sleeping Ava in her portable crib, Morgan came back frowning. She began slamming stuff with an attitude making my poor grandbaby flinch. I didn't know what had her heated, but she needed to calm down before she woke up the baby. Cocking my head to the side while massaging my chin, I watched her intently texting on her phone. She seemed to be in distress.

"You alright over there, Morgan?" I probed.

"I'm fine." She smacked her lips.

"Not by the way you're slamming stuff. Can you keep it down, please?" I was irritated.

"Excuse me? This my damn house. I pay the bills up in here. If you don't like it, feel free to leave." She pointed to the door.

"Why you always got to be difficult? A nigga was trying to see if you was straight because you seemed upset. But don't worry, I won't ask again." I took out my phone and started texting.

Morgan released a sigh and plopped down on the couch next to me as she put a pillow against her chest. She then tucked her feet underneath.

"I guess you will have to do since Eva isn't here for me to vent to, but don't be telling my business. Don't think we are cool." She frowned.

"Aight, no problem," I laughed.

"Family can be the worst. They only want to be bothered when they need something. I have two half-sisters and one brother on my sperm donor's side, who are a few years older than me. They basically never wanted a relationship with me because their father cheated with my mom and conceived me. I understand their mom got hurt, but I shouldn't be punished because of two selfish adults. She wasn't that fed up because they never divorced. Anyway, our father has a trust fund for my siblings and I that we can only receive, if we spend a week together at his choosing, but I don't want to do it. But I deserve that fuckin' money without any stipulations. He never took care of me. Occasionally, he would send a few dollars to my grandma or buy one birthday gift every couple of years, but that's about it. I was living dirt poor in Baltimore while he had his family living in a mansion," she ranted.

"You can't choose the family you're born into, but you ain't got to take their crap either. If you don't want to fake it, don't. Tell them to fuck off. They only want to be bothered with you because of the money."

"True. Enough about my family drama. I need a drink." She walked to her mini bar to make a drink.

The two of us drank an entire bottle of Tequila as baby Ava remained fast asleep. When Morgan complained about being hot, she slipped off her shirt and wore only a sports bra with her boy shorts that exposed the bottom of her cheeks. Looking at her hardened nipples, I instinctively licked my lips as my dick got hard. Our eyes connected like two magnets, and next thing I know, she was on top of me sticking her tongue in my mouth. While we were kissing, I firmly gripped her ass. Each kiss became even more intense. I forcefully gripped her ponytail and sucked on her neck while she softly moaned. I just knew I was about to get some pussy until my cockblocking granddaughter woke up crying.

A panicked Morgan leaped up off me and picked her shirt up from the floor. She placed it against her chest with a bewildered expression. As I got ready to pick up Ava to comfort her, Morgan unexpectedly shoved my duffle bag in my chest.

"Nigga, you got to get up out of here." She was fidgety and wouldn't look into my eyes.

"Calm down." I tried to grab her hand and she snatched away.

"I am calm. Now you got to go, man. Ava will be fine. If I need you, I will call or send a bat signal, shit. Just please go." She was adamant.

After rubbing my granddaughter on the cheek, I took my duffle bag and left. I didn't want to make Morgan feel uncomfortable in her own space. However, I did want to find out how her pussy felt.

Chapter Six
MORGAN REID

A blaring alarm sounded in my condo as I sat on my couch looking over client files with my cat snuggled on my lap. The abrupt noise scared him, and he sank his long claws into my thigh, making me shriek in discomfort. With haste, I scooped his furry body in my arms, running out the door, barefoot wearing only a robe. The hallway was engulfed in smoke. I couldn't help but cough and wheeze. Once I made it safely out the building, I was able to catch my breath. The fire department was on the scene to investigate what was causing the smoke.

With my cat closely cuddled to my chest, I was asking one of my neighbors if they knew what was going on in the building, but no one seemed to know anything. Then, ear hustling Vicki approached us, so we stopped talking. She was the building gossiper who loved to start drama. She tried to pat the top of my cat's head, but I wasn't having that. I almost beat her ass.

"Don't you dare put your stinky ass hands on my cat. Tink and I don't know you like that. Back your ass up." I gritted my teeth.

Vicki gasped, clutched her imaginary pearls, and kept it moving. Shortly after the fire department arrived, the news station was on the scene. A female reporter with sandy blond hair unexpectedly strolled up to a group of us holding a microphone. Out of everyone standing on the scene, she asked to interview me. Even though I looked a hot ass mess, I wasn't going to miss my opportunity to be on television.

"We are reporting live in front of this condominium where tenants had to evacuate because of a unit catching fire. I am standing here with one of them now, Morgan Weed," she said my name loud and wrong.

I snatched her microphone while still holding my cat and corrected her dinky ass.

"It's Morgan Reid, attorney at law." I smiled.

"Can you tell us what caused the fire?" she tried to get her microphone back, but I tugged it away, still looking at the camera.

"Hell if I know, lady. They better come fix this shit. I pay too much money. Me and Tinkerbell were scared for our lives." I was dramatic.

"Thank you so much for taking the time to speak with us." The reporter took her microphone back, and smiled.

"You're welcome. Hey, Eva girl. Tink and I are on tv," I shouted my boo out.

Eventually, we were cleared by the fire department to enter back in the building. One of my stupid ass neighbors forgot to turn off their space heater when they left their unit. Shaking my head in disbelief, I placed Tinkerbell on the floor and got in the shower. I had a dinner date on a Sunday with Eva and her family. Even though I truly did miss spending time with my best friend, I was happy for all the new blessings she obtained in her life.

My Lyft was waiting for me outside. I grabbed me a bottle of wine and left out the door. I hated driving in DC because the traffic was ridiculous. The smell of armpits assaulted my nostrils as I climbed in the backseat. I immediately rolled down the window to let some fresh air in the car because it smelled like a bag of onions. My eyes were watery from holding my breath, and my stomach felt sour the entire ride to Georgetown. Before the driver could pull up in front of the house and stop, I swung open the door gasping for fresh air.

Strutting towards the front door with my bottle of wine, I rang the doorbell. Eva answered it, cradling her baby in her arms wearing the biggest smile on her face. I couldn't believe my best friend was finally a mother. It warmed my heart seeing her so happy. With a huge smile on my face, I gently pulled Eva in half a hug, and then I peered down joyfully at my Goddaughter Ava, who was just so precious.

"I'm so glad to be here. I missed you." I was excited.

"You can always come here to visit. You're family. What your crazy ass been up to?" Eva probed.

I badly wanted to tell Eva about my kiss with Maino, but I knew she could care less about his ass. They barely acknowledged one another when they were in the same room anyway. It was just a simple hi and bye, that's all. Their common ground was Ace and baby Ava.

"Just working hard to make partner at the law firm. Girl, do you know my building caught fire because someone had a space heater and forgot to turn that sucka off," I explained, shaking my head.

"Really? Are you okay?" she was concerned.

"Tinkerbell and I are fine. I think my baby is still a little shaken up, though. A part of me didn't want to leave him, but he should be fine until I get back."

"You and that damn cat," she laughed. "I swear you love him more than me."

"You two don't have to fight for my love. It's enough of me to go around, baby," I joked. "Before I forget, I shouted you out on the news."

"Oh, my goodness. You're a mess. What am I going to do with you?"

I just shrugged my shoulders and followed Eva in her naturally lit kitchen. There was a spread of food sitting on the table. I quickly made my plate and walked out back to the patio where everyone was eating at the table, including that damn Maino. When he looked up from his phone with his hooded eyes on me, my core tingled. Biting the edge of my lip, I began imagining his big, strong, callous hands gripping my thighs while he hungrily ate at my pussy.

"Morgan, you okay?" the sound of Lovely's voice brought me out of my naughty thoughts.

"Yes, I'm fine, boo." I gave her a hug and smiled at her new baby girl, Ella.

I glanced around the table looking for an empty space, and there was one next to Maino. Fuck my life. Sighing heavily, I plopped down on the chair. When my leg accidentally rubbed against his, he looked up at me with his eyebrows knitted and a playful smirk on his lips.

"What's good, Morgan?" he spoke after sipping on his drink.

"My blood pressure," I joked.

"Shiddd, I know the feeling."

"Are you eating swine?" I frowned my face looking at Maino bite into his piece of ham.

"Fuck yeah. I love me a pig. Want some?" he shoved it in my face, and I gagged.

"My body is too fine and divine to eat some nasty swine."

"You ain't never lie about that." He licked his lips, staring me down with lust.

Every so often, I spotted Maino's eyes dancing back and forth between his plate and my face. From the way he kept looking at me, my body kept squirming under his intense gaze. My panties were soaked in my juices while my nipples were rock hard. When I stood up from the table and went to get me a drink, Maino followed me inside in the house. While I was searching the cabinet for a drink, he pretended to use his phone, but that nigga's mouth wasn't moving. He slipped it in his pocket before towering over me with his hands in his pockets. A huge lump formed in my throat as we locked eyes. I swallowed hard when he pushed a piece of my fallen hair out of my face.

"What? Why you keep looking at me like you're in love and shit? I know my kisses are good, but damn. Don't tell me I got to put a restraining order on you." I was sassy.

"Seriously, Morgan. I don't want things to be awkward between us. We both are grown, and we kissed. I don't mind doing it again." He glided his tongue across his lips.

My breathing hitched when Maino cupped the side of my chin and leaned down to kiss my lips. Our tongues connected as I closed my eyes, savoring the moment. I gently rubbed his back, moaning in his mouth, and he unexpectedly picked me from the floor, sitting me on the kitchen counter. While he trailed the side of my neck with kisses, the sound of loud footsteps approaching startled me, so I shoved him away. Maino scraped a hand through his sea of waves giving me a sensual look while I dropped down to fix the wrinkles in my shirt. Thank goodness Ace strolled in the kitchen holding his plate to get some more food because if he didn't, I would've been fuckin' his daddy.

Chapter Seven
MAURICE "MAINO" PIERCE

My music was blasting as I cruised down the street in my red Lamborghini, smoking a blunt. It was after one, and I was starving like a mothafucka on my way to get something to eat. When I pulled up to one of my favorite spots down Florida Avenue, my phone began ringing. Looking down at my screen, I saw it was my girlfriend, Winter. We were on and off for three years. Our relationship was toxic, so I preferred to stay out in the streets making my money than going home.

"What it do?" I answered.

"What time are you coming home?" she was being nosy.

"I don't know." I was being honest.

Winter stayed monitoring my calls and whereabouts like she was a fuckin' warden. That shit was a huge turn-off.

"We need to talk." She smacked her lips.

"That's cool. Whenever I get home, we'll talk." I ended the call.

I climbed out my car and strolled in the restaurant. There was a woman standing in front of me with a long ass ponytail that reached down to her phat ass. When she turned around from the counter, I immediately laughed because it was Morgan's ass I was looking at.

"What's good, Morgan? What you doing in here, around this area?" her face was frowned up.

"Go head, roach before I spray you with some raid. We are not cool." She was feisty.

"Yeah, I forgot you was my biggest hater." I shook my head, chuckling.

"Boy bye. Nobody is hating on your tired ass." She pursed her lips.

"Aight, whatever you say, ashy feet." I was trying to set her off.

"Oh no. Nothing on me is ashy, baby. You wish whatever gorilla you laid up with looked as good as me." She seemed offended.

I knew she was going to get annoyed.

"You aight. You ain't all that." I was messing with her.

"Nigga, please. Even a blind man can see how fine I am." She posed with her hands on her thighs.

The cashier at the counter called Morgan's order number, and she grabbed her food. Before she strutted out the door with her big, black shades above her eyes, she looked me up and down with her upper lip curved. I watched her switch those thick hips and big ass out the door.

After getting my food, I drove home, and Winter was sitting in the living room sipping a drink. I greeted her with a head nod. Then she lobbed a champagne glass at my head. With a scowl on my face, I managed to duck out the way. I didn't know what the fuck was her issue. She wanted a reaction out of me real hard, but I wasn't going to give her that satisfaction of control. I was staring at her momentarily shaking my head and walking to my master bedroom. I had only taken about three steps and she came from behind me, punching me on my back, sobbing. Hitting a woman wasn't my thing, so I kept my hands to myself as I let her wail away at my back until she became exhausted. With her back up against the wall, she slid down to the floor, trembling.

"I don't know what your problem is but putting your hands on me isn't called for. If it was another nigga, they would've whooped your ass," I spoke through gritted teeth.

"Fuck you, Maino! You are just like those dog ass cheating niggas. I'm sick of you stepping on me. If you keep it up, I'm leaving you this time. I have so many other niggas who want me, but I'm too stuck on your ass." She was angry.

"Go, Winter. I ain't asking you to fuckin' stay. I don't have to be in a relationship with you to be a father to my daughter." I was blunt.

"Please, once I am done with you, your connections with law enforcement are over." She called herself threatening me.

"Bitch, your father works for me. I'm calling the shots." I had to remind her.

"I'll see about that, Maino." She picked up her phone.

I chuckled watching Winter talking with her father on speaker, trying to get him to put me in my place. He didn't do shit but tell her to stop making trouble. That nigga didn't want any problems with me. I knew too many of Commissioner Pratt's skeletons.

* * *

Three Weeks Later...

Claps and whistles erupted in the auditorium as my daughter, Mira, walked on the stage to receive her high school diploma. Her mother, Layla was standing next to me dabbing her cheeks with a tissue, so I pulled her into a hug, making her smile. We had been separated for years because I couldn't keep my dick in my pants, but she made our co-parenting relationship easy. Even after she got married and had other children, we always stayed solid. After the ceremony, we gathered outside, and Mira walked out the school building holding her cap and gown, wearing a white dress with her hair flowing down her back, looking just like an angel. When she saw me standing there holding twelve stem roses, she ran through a group of people, leaping into my arms and giving me the tightest hug before kissing my cheek.

"I'm proud of you, Ms. Valedictorian." I kissed her forehead and handed her the roses.

"Thank you, dad. Now, where is my car?" she grinned.

"What car?" I played it off.

"Really? You told me when I graduated, you were going to get me a car," she reminded me.

"Aight, what type of car?" I probed, raising my eyebrow.

"What's my budget? That will help me narrow down my options." She batted her eyelashes.

"No budget. You can have any car you want as long as your mother approves," I explained.

Although I enjoyed spoiling my daughter with lavish gifts, I always wanted to be on the same page with her mother. If she didn't approve, I didn't step on her toes because Mira lived with her primarily.

"Well, in that case, I want a BMW SUV. I'm trying to stunt like my daddy." She was hyped.

I looked at her mother for the final answer, and she nodded her in approval with a smirk on her face. After taking a few pictures, Mira and I climbed in my BMW before zooming out the parking lot. We cranked up the go-go music as the both of us drove around the city cruising with the drop top-down stunting. Our first stop was at Tysons Corner Mall, where I gave her my black card so she could get whatever she wanted. Then, we went to eat at Joe's Seafood Prime Steak & Stone Crab. It was a fancy little spot on Pennsylvania Avenue, Downtown, DC. It was like butter cutting into my porterhouse steak. The waitress was even better though. When she came to refill our water glasses, I realized how fat her ass was, and she caught me. I thought I was about to get cursed out or accused of being a pervert, but she slipped me her number under the table on a strip of paper on my thigh.

"That's a shame, dad. Everywhere we go, you're booking somebody. I'm going to need you to settle down, old man." Mira shook her head.

"Old man? I am only thirty-eight. I'm in my prime." I drank some water.

"Okay, Mac daddy. You being in your prime got you a three year old and a clingy baby mama. How is Winter anyway? I bet she is still acting like Blue's Clues trying find out if you're cheating," Mira laughed and joked.

It was no secret that I enjoyed the company of beautiful women. Long-term relationships just weren't my thing. Winter hated that about me, but it's not like she didn't know. I told her how I rolled. I guess she thought she could change me, but I told her not to get her feelings involved. She snuck in my phone one day and saw naked pictures of different women. We got into an argument and she started giving me ultimatums to cut my roster loose. She wanted a ring, so I told her ass to bounce. The only thing we needed to discuss was how we were going to amicably co-parent our three-year-old daughter, Nova.

"We broke up," I revealed.

I couldn't love Winter the way she desired. Shit, I didn't even love myself. My love only ran deep for my kids.

"That woman really thought she was going to change you. It's going to take a straight firecracker to put you in your place. Lord, I can't wait to see that," she chuckled.

"Believe me, if it does happen, that'll be a miracle." I smirked and shoved a nice juicy piece of tender steak in my mouth.

"You never know; that may be soon." She grinned.

"You crazy, girl. Finish your food." I smiled.

"I sure am, but you love me." She sang.

"With my whole heart." I looked her in her eyes.

We finished eating our food, and I paid for the check.

Pulling up to her mother's house, we stepped out my car. Mira was eyeballing the shit out of the silver BMW SUV that had a big red bow on the grill parked in the driveway. I was saving the best gift for last. When I pulled out the key fob from my pants pocket, and placed it into her hand, tears sprung from her hazel eyes. She gave me the biggest hug and couldn't stop saying that I was the best dad in the world. All I lived for was to make my kids happy.

I gave my daughter one last hug and hopped in my ride to Ace's house for poker night. We were sitting down at a circulator table talkin' shit while Morgan strutted down in the basement holding a beer. Eva was visiting her parents for dinner, so I didn't understand why she was there. When Morgan sat down on the chair next to me, I slammed my eyebrows together curiously.

"Wingo couldn't make it, so we needed another person," Ace told me.

"It doesn't matter to me, as long as she got the paper." I shrugged.

"Fool, you ain't saying nothing but a word. I'm ready to take y'all money. Mama got to buy a new pair of dildos," Morgan joked.

"Aye, man. Nobody wants to hear about you buying no plastic dicks." Easton frowned.

"That explains a lot," I chuckled.

"Excuse me, Maurice?" she cut her eyes at me.

"It's Maino," I corrected her.

"Umhum." She pursed her lips.

Smirking, Morgan pulled two stacks out of her big ass purse, slamming them on the table, picked up the deck of cards, and began shuffling them like she was a Vegas dealer. We played several individual rounds before pairing up as teams and raising the stakes. I had loudmouth Morgan.

On our last deal, we bet the entire money pot. The last person to show their hand was Morgan and she had a royal flush. She placed her hands on top of the money, pulling it in her direction like it wasn't a team effort.

"What do you think you're doing? That ain't all your money." I looked her up and down.

"Oh yeah, don't worry. I'm a give you your cut. Let me pay you for your partnership." Morgan took out a twenty-dollar bill from the pile of money and scooped the rest of the money in her big ass Louis Vuitton purse.

"It's always good seeing you East and Ace." She smiled at them.

"Nice to see you too, Morgan." I was being sarcastic.

"Yea whatever, Mango," she laughed and left.

Chapter Eight
MORGAN REID

Playing poker against those fools was like taking candy from a baby. With my purse hiked on my shoulder, I strutted towards my truck, ready to go to the mall to spend their money. As I clicked on my key fob to unlock it, Maino jogged in my direction. He unexpectedly gripped my arm and pinned me against the driver's door. Using his index finger, he trailed down my neck as I pushed out a slow breath. I hated the way my body lost control in his presence.

"What the hell do you think you're doing?" I did my best to bite back my smile.

"Coming to get my share of the money. You weren't playing by yourself." He tugged on my purse.

I cocked my head slightly to the side and smirked, "I already gave you your cut. Now you better take your little funky twenty dollars and get out my face."

"Aight, if you ain't trying to give me none of the money, then at least give me a kiss." He smirked deviously.

"Hell no." I shook my head.

"Why do you got to play hard to get, Morgan? You know you're feeling me as much as I'm feeling you. Now stop fronting and give me a kiss. If you behave, I will kiss your other set of lips." He sucked on my earlobe.

My panties became drenched, and I was ready to lay in the backseat of my truck with my ass hovering in the air to receive his dick. I bet he had the type of stroke game that would have me washing out his dirty draws. No thanks!

"Nope, your breath probably smells like booty juice." I kept playing hard to get.

Yea, his breath was fresh, but he had to earn what I had to give.

I shook my head in disbelief watching Maino pull out Listerine strips from his pants pocket, placing them onto his tongue. When he cupped my chin, I just gave in, melted into his arms and let him kiss me. That moment was soooo intense. Tongue, tongue, and more tongue. I needed to get away from him. My knees were getting weak. He had me gliding my hands down his back and moaning into his mouth. The only reason why we separated our lips was because someone cleared their throat. Frantically, I pushed Maino on his chest away from me and turned around to see Easton recording us on his phone with a damn smirk. Letting my guard down, I got caught slipping. He had me hot. Maino was standing there grinning like a Pekingese, rubbing his chin.

When I rushed towards Easton to take his phone, his childish ass ran around my truck. I knew from the devious look in his eyes, we were gonna have to pay to keep his mouth shut. I didn't have time for something less than foreplay to be turned into some kind of sex scandal in Washington DC. Mothafuckas were freaky as shit in the city! My actions were careless. The worst part was, Maino had me doing stupid stuff, and he didn't even dick me down.

"I ain't the type of nigga to blackmail, but I know a lot of people would find this video funny," Easton laughed.

"How much for you to erase the video?" I bargained.

"I ain't paying that nigga shit." Maino didn't seem too thrilled about his proposition.

"All I need is the poker money." Easton stuck out his hand.

"You son of a bitch," I mumbled and took the money out my purse.

After Easton erased the video from his phone and iCloud, he

tossed us a head nod climbing into his car before speeding down the street with my damn money. I punched Maino on his arm, and he laughed with his hand against his mouth.

"Now we both are out of money because you can't keep your lips to yourself, fool." I pouted and stomped my feet.

"We? You weren't sharing it with me. Remember you told me to take my funky ass twenty dollars. Now look at you, broke. I still got mine, though." He pulled the twenty dollars I had given him out of his pocket with a smug grin.

I snatched it from his hand, tore it up into small pieces, and tossed it at his face, "Now we both out of money. See you around, big head."

I got in my truck and drove back to my office to work on some cases. My ass was supposed to be at lunch, but I was playing poker. While I looked through some legal documents, I ordered Thai food to be delivered. It was my favorite thing to eat, but it didn't always agree with my stomach. After eating, my stomach felt so full I had to unloosen my around my slacks. Soon afterwards, my eyes began to feel heavy. I had the itis. Yawning, I locked my office door and relaxed on my leather couch, closing my eyes for a slight nap.

* * *

Being an attorney was a rewarding job, but it also got super stressful. After a long day at the office dealing with stupid ass clients, I was craving to get high. The right side of my temple was throbbing. I kicked my heels off by the door and slammed my purse on my counter before heading straight to my bedroom to get my stash. I grabbed my first aid kit from underneath my bed and sat down on the floor Indian style with my dick bong out. As I got ready to be on cloud nine, I heard a knock on my apartment door. Looking through the peephole, I saw it was my Uncle Courtney. A smile emerged on my lips. I opened the door, and he was on his cellphone cursing out his boyfriend, Martell. I couldn't stand his man because he was on the downlow. I didn't understand how my uncle could be denied in public and only accepted in the bedroom. Even though that shit made me hot, it wasn't my business to understand.

"Let me call you back. I'm at my people's house," Courtney hung up and focused his attention on me, "Bitch, what took you so long? I almost broke a damn nail."

"Nobody didn't tell you to pop up at my place. You lucky I answered the door. Next time I'm gonna leave you out here knocking," I joked.

"Try if you want to, Morgan, and I'm gonna to set it off up in this bitch. You know I don't play, alright." He snaked his neck.

"Watch me. I bet Karen gonna call the police on your black ass too. I would tell you not to drop the soap, but you will like that," I joked and plopped on my couch.

"Don't let living around these white people get you acting cute. I will kick your ass." He swung his beautiful locks from out his face.

I dropped my head, laughing at my uncle. We were only two years apart, so I damn sure didn't take him seriously. He wouldn't even hurt a damn fly. My fluffy bear was gentle.

"What brings you here uninvited?" I waited for him to speak.

Releasing a sigh, Courtney got comfortable on my couch, crossing his legs, showing off his beautiful red bottoms. I prayed he wasn't there to talk about our crazy family. Honestly, I wasn't in the mood to deal with the dysfunction. If they weren't fighting or trashing each other on social media, they were judging you for not being holy enough. The only time I had the energy to tolerate the Reids was on holidays. I only could do that in small doses. If it wasn't for my uncle begging me to show my face, I damn sure wouldn't visit.

"I hate to ask you, but you're the only person who can help me. Can I borrow two thousand dollars? I promise to give it back next month. Please, Pooh. It's urgent," he sighed, "Martell owes Maino, and if he doesn't pay by tomorrow, he's making a house call."

Rage shot throughout my body, and I slammed my bong on the floor, shattering it. Courtney's body jumped as he placed his hand on his racing chest. He should've known I would react that way about his dumb ass down low boyfriend. He was a straight up weed head who spent more time playing his video game than hustling on the damn block. I couldn't stand that son of a bitch but tolerated him because of my uncle. Nonetheless, I was no longer holding my tongue to protect his feelings when his little boy toy was putting his life in danger. Love and hard dick made people lose their damn minds.

"You expect me to give my hard earned money to a man who doesn't want to work? Hell no!" I yelled.

"He does work," Courtney defended him, and it pissed me off.

"Selling dime bags from the window of y'all small ass apartment ain't working. Now, come again? He's a got damn bum!" I yelled.

"Listen, Morgan. I know you don't understand it, but I love this man. I would be devastated if something happens to him. He already has a broken hand. I can imagine what that nigga Maino is gonna do next. Can you please let me borrow the money? You know I'm good for it."

"When do you need the money?" I folded my arms across my chest.

"Maino is bringing one of his men to collect it tomorrow at noon," he sighed.

"Fine, I will be there. I need to make sure you don't get screwed or die trying to protect that no good bum." I was so angry.

"Oh, no, Morgan," he popped his lips. "It's risky that I even came to you in the first place for help because of your job. You are the only person I could ask for help, but you can't be there with us." He was worried.

"It's not up for discussion. Either I can be there, or you can get the money another way, but the choice is up to you. How I see it, you don't have many options." I was blunt.

My uncle reluctantly agreed and left without joining me for a smoke session. I got comfortable on the couch with my other dick bong placing it against my mouth. When I finished smoking, I had the munchies and drove to get me something to eat from McDonald's. The drive-thru line expanded past the entrance into the street. Still, ordering inside wasn't an option. I looked a hot ass mess with my bonnet on my head and grandma pajamas that I was wearing. After waiting in the damn line forever, it was finally my turn to order, and the heffa who was running the drive-thru had an attitude like she didn't want to be at work. She kept smacking her lips and huffing every time I told her what I wanted. Even though her customer service was some trash, I let it go because anyone could have a bad day, including me. However, when I pulled up to pay, that bitch snatched my bank card from my hand. It was on and popping. I snatched it right back before pointing my finger in her face.

"I don't know what your issue is, but you need to calm all that down. Don't you ever snatch anything from me," I spoke through my gritted teeth.

"Bruh, you are tripping. I didn't snatch anything from you." The girl rolled her eyes.

She looked like she was in her mid-twenties.

"Bruh? Do I look like a man to you? Little girl, where is your manager? Your customer service sucks." I felt myself about to get out my truck and climb through the tiny ass window and grab her fuckin' neck.

"The same place your mama is, in hell." She put her middle finger up at me and slammed the drive-thru window.

That bitch had the right one because I didn't give a fuck about whooping somebody's ass and their dusty ass ma. Parking my truck, I stormed in the McDonald's demanding to see a manager. His fat stinky ass approached the counter sweating profusely with a nasty looking shirt on that had a million stains on it. He was out of breath the moment he opened his mouth.

"What seems to be the problem, ma'am?" he smiled, showing his nasty ass teeth that looked like it was covered in butter.

"The problem is the person you got running the drive-thru is rude as hell. She called herself snatching my card. I don't appreciate that. You better get her before I go back there and beat her ass. I ain't the one." I cracked my knuckles.

I didn't give a shit about being an attorney. That was only a title and I was from the streets. I refused to get disrespected by some nappy-headed heffa with some dry-looking bundles. Bitch please.

"That's not necessary. We truly apologize for the situation. We are happy to take your order here and compensate you for the trouble." He was trying to make up for his employee being a bitch.

"I don't need your hand out. I can pay for my own meals. You better just get her because if I come in here again, I am leaving in handcuffs." I rolled my eyes.

I stepped up to the register, and a petite young lady with curly long hair greeted me with a smile and took my order. She even repeated it back to me before swiping my card. Her customer service skills were top notch. While I waited for my food, I went to fill my cup up with soda and saw that damn Maino tucked away in the back sitting at a booth drinking coffee. It was no coincidence. He was stalking me. That sucka probably had one of his workers put a tracker under my truck. Shaking the thought out my head, I placed my hands on my hips and approached him. Clearing my throat, he lifted his head up from the newspaper he was reading. He slowly raked his eyes down my body making me feel exposed.

"I knew I recognized your loud ass voice. I see you out here showing your ass," he chuckled.

"No, I'm not. That little bitch in the drive-thru messing with me. What the hell are you doing here anyway? You following me?" I accused and pursed my lips.

Maino hit me with a smirk and my clit jumped. She had been betraying me whenever he was in my presence. I tightly clenched my thighs together.

"Hell naw, I ain't no stalker. I'm waiting for my daughter to get off so I can drive her home."

"Hold up. You making all that money and got your poor baby working? You ain't shit." I shook my head and then took a sip of my soda.

"She ain't got to work, but she wants to. My baby girl is independent and headstrong," he laughed.

"I hope your daughter ain't the one working the drive-thru." I was lowkey embarrassed.

"Naw, she ain't because you're still breathing," he laughed, but I knew part of him was serious.

What parent wouldn't be?

My order number was called, so I went to grab my food. That's when I spotted the young lady who took my order approaching Maino holding a bag of food. He immediately pulled her into his arms and kissed her forehead. She playfully wiped it off before sticking out her tongue. They made their way to his BMW and I found myself watching them. I could tell Maino was a wonderful father.

*　*　*

I panicked, leaping from my bed after seeing the time, and rushed in my closet, putting on some clothes before bolting out the house. Maino would be sending one of his men to collect his money, so I wanted to meet him at his funeral home to convince him to give Martell some more time. Yes, I had the money, but I didn't feel like I should have to pay for someone else's fuck up. When I pulled in the front of the building, I grabbed my purse and climbed out my truck. A receptionist was sitting at the front desk typing on her computer.

"Hi, may I help you?" she immediately greeted me with a smile.

"Um, yes. Is Maino here?"

"Is Mr. Pierce expecting you?" she eyed me suspiciously.

"No, but it's urgent."

"I see. Let me see if I can get a hold of him. Mr. Pierce isn't supposed to be here today. You can take a seat." She smiled.

"Tell him it's Morgan," I called out.

I took a seat and glanced around the lobby. As the receptionist talked lowly on the phone, she looked at me. She then nodded her head before ending the call.

"He's not available. You can leave your number and I will give it to him." She searched for something on her desk.

I wrote my number on her notepad and got ready to get up to leave when Maino came out in the lobby talking on his cellphone. His nostrils were flaring while his chest thrust out. After rolling my eyes at the lying receptionist, who was probably fuckin' him, I approached him with a smile, but he didn't return one. He just towered over me with his dark hooded eyes. From his cold demeanor, I wasn't dealing with Maurice the man. It was Maino the kingpin.

Chapter Nine
MAURICE "MAINO" PIERCE

I towered over Morgan with my jaws locked and could tell she was uncomfortable. She just popped up at the wrong time, so I didn't have time to talk. I just received a call that my worker got pulled over because of a busted tail light. When they searched his car, he had a few bricks in the trunk. He immediately began talking, trying to cut him a deal by telling the two officers he got the product from me, not knowing they were on my payroll. I didn't respect any man who would cooperate with the FEDs to save their own asses.

"Why did you have your receptionist lie to me knowing you were here? If you were busy, all you had to do was say that, Maino. You didn't have to lie." Morgan seemed upset, "I just need to talk with you about something and it can't wait."

"Go head and talk." I stuck my hands into my pockets.

"I prefer if we talk about this in private." She looked behind her shoulder at my receptionist.

I motioned for Morgan to follow me to my office. She took a seat and I sat on the edge of my desk. For some reason she looked a mess, but I still found her attractive. She brought up my worker Martell owing me some money because I spotted him. She explained the only reason why she knew here was because her uncle was dating him, but I had to promise not to fire him since she outed that he was gay. I didn't discriminate, especially when money was involved. And besides, I already knew he was gay because he was my baby mama, Winter's, cousin.

"How about Martell gives you a thousand dollars today and another thousand next week?" Please?" she begged.

"For you, I will do it. But after that, I am breaking some necks." His nostrils flared.

"You won't have to do that. Come by my place tonight, and I will give you a thousand today, but it has to be before eight. Eva and I are going to a party tonight."

"Just make sure you put that nasty cat in the cage." I frowned.

"Whatever, you better leave my Tink alone." She smiled.

I was deeply engrossed in my conversation that I almost didn't hear my cell ringing. Looking down at my screen, I saw it was Rich. I kissed Morgan on the forehead, promising to meet up later before strutting out my funeral home. I climbed in Rich's truck and we made our way to the snitch's crib. Just like we thought, he was packing shit in his duffle bag when we kicked down his back door. His eyes widened before tossing the bag at us and trying to flee. He was free to run all he wanted, but I never met a man who could outrun bullets. I sent two shots in the back of his legs, causing him to drop to his knees. He began using his hands to crawl as we towered over him, aiming our guns at his head.

"Did you really think your bitch ass was gonna snitch on me and escape town?" I kicked him on the side of his ribs.

"Please, Maino don't kill me, man. I didn't tell no cops anything, man. You got it all wrong. They were pressing me about you. I ain't tell them shit though." He looked at me with pleading eyes.

Rich kept his gun trained on him while I went in his kitchen, holding a bag to whip up a special meal for him. As I sat at the table, baring my teeth and pointing my gun, I glared at my worker, Deshawn, shoving pieces of cut-up rat meat in his mouth. He sobbed through every swallow knowing it would be his last meal. When he began throwing up, I stood up and struck him with the butt of his gun, busting open his nose. Then I grabbed the back of his head, slamming it into his vomit, making him eat it. He pleaded for his life, but I didn't give a fuck. I silenced him dead. His head dropped on the plate full of rat meat and entrails.

"A rat for a rat. Call the clean-up crew to come get this nigga and wipe everything down," I told Rich.

"Done." Rich nodded.

"Did you put money on J- Rock books?" I probed.

J-Rock was the one who taught me about the drug game. I started out as his second in command before he got locked up after some cop who used to work on our team planted drugs in his house. He ended up getting ten years.

"It's taken care of and I paid his mom dukes too," he assured me.

J- Rock was supposed to be getting out in the next few months, so I wanted to make sure I got everything set up for him. I knew he was going to want to get back to pushing weight, and I didn't have a problem with that. I had already made arrangements. However, I wasn't giving him my top spot and wasn't demoting Rich either. He was my eyes and ears. Together, we had created a lucrative drug empire.

A few hours later, I went to Morgan's condo. I was expecting her to be already dressed up for her event, but she was wearing a fluffy pink robe with rollers in her hair. She allowed me inside, and I made myself comfortable on her couch, while she looked down at her phone with a frown. She tossed it to the side, releasing a sigh.

"I can't believe this shit," she mumbled.

"You good?" I probed.

"No, I'm pissed. Apparently, Ace has food poisoning and now Eva can't come with me to my cousin's party on my father's side. She doesn't have anybody to watch the baby. Now I have to go alone. I don't want to be in the same room with my sperm donor's other kids. Not unless you want to come with me?" she smiled.

"Naw, I don't do parties." I shook my head.

"Please, I will owe you big. I really don't want to go alone," Morgan pouted and begged.

When Morgan leaped on top of me giving me kisses, I knew she was desperate. I eventually gave in and called in a favor to get me a suit to bring it to her place. Never in my life have I went out my way to appease any woman, but Morgan. I found myself breaking my own rules. As I fixed my tie, Morgan strutted out wearing a gold gown showcasing her bodacious curves. I licked my lips, checking her out from head to toe. I had to adjust my hard dick. After feeding her ugly ass cat, Tink, who kept trying to rub on me, we got into the stretch limo. During the ride, she looked out the window in silence. She had never been that quiet. I decided to check-in. I rubbed her leg, and she looked up at me with a faint smile.

"Why you so quiet?" I rubbed her chin.

"I really don't want to go to this party, but I promised my cousin, Yara. She is the only person who deals with me on my father's side," she revealed. "I'm really not in the mood to see my siblings."

"Fuck those people. We are gonna eat up the food and drink up all their liquor." I tried to make her laugh, and it worked.

Our limo pulled up in front of the hotel, and I climbed out first before extending my hand to Morgan. The flashing lights from photographer cameras flickered nonstop as we walked in the ballroom. When I placed my gigantic hand on the arch of her back while we momentarily posed, I could feel her body reacting to my touch. We were escorted to a table that was under a golden chandelier. The waitress dressed in all black took our order as a heavy-set woman with cinnamon-brown skin and long eyelashes approached us smiling. She immediately pulled Morgan into a hug before setting her sights on me, smiling.

"Diva, I'm so glad you can make it." She kissed her cheek.

"Of course, I wouldn't miss your party. This is Maino." Morgan introduced me with a smile and kept her hand on my shoulder.

"What's good? Nice to meet you." I extended my hand and she firmly shook it.

As we were talking with Yara, I noticed that Morgan's attention was somewhere else and saw she was looking at a table. There were two women and a dude sipping on drinks, while mugging Morgan down. I waited until her cousin walked away to greet more guests. Then, I circled my arm around Morgan's waist to whisper in her ear.

"Who is those people giving you dirty looks? Do you want me to go over there to address them?" I spoke through my gritted teeth.

"Those are my siblings. Ignoring me as usual but giving me dirty looks. Hey, I'm used to it," she sighed.

I placed my hand on Morgan to give her comfort as she drank her champagne. It had to be a messed-up feeling to be denied for something you didn't have any control over. The two of us stayed closely together, just chilling and vibing.

Chapter Ten
MORGAN REID

Watching Maino interact with people at the party, I couldn't help but keep a smile on my face. He was very charming and knew how to lead a conversation regardless of the topic. Every so often, he would pull my body close to his and whisper in my ear to see if I was okay. Despite all the dirty looks from my siblings, I felt secure.

"Do you want another drink?" Maino looked down at my empty champagne glass.

"That would be great. Thank you." I smiled.

"Alright, I'll be right back."

Maino strutted towards the bar holding our empty champagne glasses, and I could see women's eyes drifting in his direction. He was a good-looking man, so I completely understood why he had a bunch of admirers. After returning with our drinks, he placed his right hand securely on the arch of my back and brushed his lips against mine. While sipping on my champagne, my breathing hitched as my chest slowly rose up and down with my heart racing. He cuffed the side of my cheek, gliding his tongue into the slit of my mouth. I tightly closed my eyes to savor the moment before melting into his arms. Deeper and deeper his tongue explored my mouth. I enjoyed it.

"How about we leave here and go back to my place to have a few more drinks?" I asked, taking another sip of champagne.

"We can go to my vacation house in Delaware. It's quiet and I have a wine cellar."

"Let me find out I already got you smitten that you want to take me away, Big Maino. I ain't mad at you. Wine and dine me, baby." I winked.

"I'm gonna show you how a real man courts a woman." He smiled.

I tossed back the champagne I had in my glass without enjoying the taste and placed it on a waiter's tray. Maino entwined his fingers in mine before we started walking towards the door to leave the event. That's when my older sister, Candice, finally approached me to start some mess. She cocked her head to the side, baring her teeth. I didn't take lightly to people sizing me up and balled up my fist.

"Is there any reason why you're standing in my way?" I looked her up and down as she smirked.

"I don't understand why you should get any of my father's money. There is no way I am going to allow it. You're a bastard who shouldn't have been born. I wish he would've flushed you down the toilet in that condom. You're trash, and so is your whore mama." I could tell she was tipsy.

"Bitch, I will beat your saddity ass. You got the right one, hoe." I snatched off my earrings.

"Bring it on, hoodrat." She pointed her finger in my face.

With a deep scowl penetrating my face, I kicked off my heel to bust her in the head with it. She leaped back, shielding her face. Just like I thought, a straight punk. When Maino scooped me into his arms, I kept kicking my feet so he could put me down. Eventually, I stopped trying to fight and laid my head on his solid chest, allowing my tears to flow. Ever since I was a kid, they always made me feel like the black sheep. I was a victim too. There were so many whispers about my mother being with a married man at my grandmother's church from the congregation. I had to endure dirty looks too.

We settled into the limo after giving the driver our destination. I laid my head on Maino's leg, sobbing. He gently rubbed his hand through my scalp. I momentarily closed my eyes to collect my thoughts before lifting my head up with teardrops on my cheeks.

"Why didn't you let me knock that hoe out? I didn't like the way she was trying to come for me. The next time I see that bitch, I'ma whoop her ass."

"Fighting isn't going to resolve your issue. It will make things worse and cause more tension. You got too much to lose. You don't want to lose your job."

"I know, but it will make me feel better," I pouted.

"After the smoke clears, you're still gonna feel upset about how your siblings treated you. The way I see it, they are trying to defend their mama's honor because she got cheated on, while you're trying to defend your character because of your mother's mistake. I don't care if you were a product of an affair; your father had an obligation to be there for you emotionally and financially, just like he was there for his other kids and his wife.

The moment she chose to stay in their marriage, she should've accepted you. However, she rather blame your mother, but not take an issue with the man who took vows to be faithful. If nobody ever told you, you are not a mistake. Your purpose was to be here. Too bad your father missed out on being a part of your life, but it's his loss." He gave me comfort.

"You don't know how bad I needed to hear that. Thank you," my voice cracked.

I gripped Maino by the tie and pulled him to my lips. He wrapped his arms around my shoulders, snuggling me close as we drove to his vacation home.

Three hours later...

Skinny dipping with Maino wasn't a good idea, but after several drinks, I found myself inside his heated pool. His lips were covering mine as he gripped my ass. I wanted more than anything for him to fuck me. However, when he pulled his lips away from mine and climbed out the water, I was confused. I waited for him to return, but he never came back outside. Sighing, I gripped the bars of the pool steps before climbing out the water to put on my dress that was laying on the lounge chair. I didn't take lightly to him ditching me like some random jump off and searched around his place to confront him. He had a nerve to be fully dressed, sitting in his man cave smoking a blunt on one of his reclining chairs in front of a big screen. I marched up to him, scowling with my hands on my hips. He looked up at me high as a kite.

"What the hell was that about, Maino? You had me butt naked and horny. I was willing to give you this pussy. You leave to go smoke. Either you're gay or a fool. From how hard your dick was, I don't think you're playing for the other team. Tell me what the fuck is wrong?" I ranted.

"Naw, it's not that. I ain't trying to hurt you, Morgan." He pushed out a sigh.

"What do you mean? You haven't hurt me?"

"I'm a dog. I don't want to do you like I do these other women. I ain't never been faithful. You're too good of a person to play games with. I rather be up front before we move any further."

"I appreciate you being honest, but I am not looking to settle down either. My career is thriving, and I love being single. Being in a relationship takes too much work. I am in a selfish phase. I don't want to worry about anyone except me. Now, if things change between us, we can cross that road when we get there, but in the meantime, I just like your company."

"Let me find out you like me more than you're showing? I knew you was feeling me." He smirked cockily.

"I do. You're kind of cute," I admitted.

"Cute? I ain't no puppy," he chuckled.

"Alright, you're sexy but don't tell anybody. I will deny it."

"I thought you were beautiful the first time I saw you on Howard's campus, even though you were about to kick my ass for knocking the books out your hands."

"What's not to like about me? I am sexy and successful. Any man would be lucky to have my attention. You have it, so don't ruin it." I caressed the side of his cheek.

"Can I taste you?" he nibbled on my ear.

"Yes, but let me go freshen up."

"Naw, I want to taste you in your natural state."

A smirk spread across his lips as he extended his gigantic hand in my direction. I hesitantly placed mine into his before he walked me upstairs to a dimly lit bedroom. Laying back on the bed, he pushed the hems of my dress above my knees and then used his index fingers to push my panties to the side. He eagerly feasted on my pussy. Closing my eyes, I fisted the silk bedsheet. A blazing orgasm ripped through my body, and I released a loud scream as tears eased from the corner of my eyes. Maino raised up his head with my juices still rolling down his cheek and kissed my lips. I loved that nasty shit.

"Tasting your good ass pussy worked up my appetite. You hungry?" he presented me with a lopsided smile.

"I am, but I don't feel like going out to eat. Let's order something from Postmates."

"I can go for a delicious omelet with cheese. Ohhh, and some blueberry pancakes from IHOP." I licked my lips and touched my growling belly.

"Go get in the shower and I will take care of the food," he assured me and kissed the center of my forehead, making me blush.

"I'll pass on the shower. I am going to test out your tub. It looks comfortable."

"There should be a robe hanging on the door. You can use that when you're done."

"Negro, I am not putting on another woman's robe. You must be tripping." I shot him a dirty look.

He laughed, shaking his head, "Those are new robes. I bought them for my daughter Mira. She hasn't worn them yet."

"Oh, my bad. You know I stay tripping sometimes." My cheeks became hot from embarrassment.

"I don't pay you any mind. You just need a real man to keep you in line."

"Every man who has tried to tame me has failed miserably." I pursed my lips.

"I'm up for the challenge, Ms. Reid."

Directly in front of Maino, I pulled my dress over my head,

showing all of my goods. He lustfully roamed my body while licking his lips. Then, he walked to me, palming my ass. I stood on my tippy toes and licked his neck before leaving him with a hard dick poking through his sweatpants. After blowing him a kiss, I shut the bathroom door and ran me some water inside the stone resin bathtub. My body immediately relaxed in the bubble bath. As I was washing my body, I heard a slight knock on the door. Maino stuck his head in but not to be on no freaky or creep shit. He had a glass of champagne and handed it to me.

"Take your time and relax. I'll be downstairs if you need me."

I wrapped my lips around the rim of the crystal glass, taking down the smooth drink. After relaxing for a bit, I continued to wash up and got out the water. With my hair still damped, I slipped the comfy Versace robe over my body and made my way downstairs. The smell of blueberry engrossed my nostrils. There was a man in the kitchen flipping pancakes with a spatula.

"What's all this, Maino?" I was in awe looking at all the food spread out on the countertop.

"You wanted breakfast and I made it happen. This is Chef Burk. We go way back."

"Nice to meet you." The chef smiled.

"A private chef for little ole me?"

"I like to take care of people who are good to me."

I walked to the table that was already set with square plates and silverware. When I got ready to pull out my own seat, Maino rushed over to do it for me. The two of us ate our food and talked. We didn't even get any sleep because we stayed up just hanging out. I swore we watched over twenty movies on Netflix. Maino had his driver come scoop us and to take me back to my place. He planned to spend some more time with me. That was until he received a call about his youngest daughter not feeling well, so he needed to leave. I honestly felt sad but understood he had to be on his daddy duties. Before he left out the door, he gave me a long, sensual kiss and then climbed in his SUV. Never in my life had I felt so protected, nurtured, and spoiled. I couldn't believe it was from Maino... A deadly Kingpin from DC.

Chapter Eleven
MAURICE "MAINO" PIERCE

I sat on the floor with my back leaned against the wall bobbing my head to my new walk-man. It was a gift from Jason for my fourteenth birthday. He got it with the money he earned from his after school job as a tutor. And although he was only two years older than me, he took on the role as my parental figure. Our pops, Michael, was in and out of prison, so he wasn't around much. Nonetheless, when he did see us, he was cool and always tried to give us advice about being good men and making something of our lives. Unfortunately, his life lessons to give to us were cut short because he died from a drug overdose. I couldn't say I loved the man, but I did have some type of respect for him. My hoe ass crackhead mother, Sarah, she was an abusive junkie ass bitch. All she cared about was sticking a needle in her arm, fuckin' random niggas for money, and screwing her children up mentally.

I kept listening to music until Jason entered our tiny bedroom we shared, holding a homemade cake. A smile immediately emerged on my lips. He always went out his way to show me love.

"Happy fourteenth Birthday Maurice," Jason smiled and handed me the homemade cake.

"You made this for me? You didn't have to man, but I really appreciate it," I felt myself getting choked up, but held back my tears.

"Anything for you little bro," he patted me on my shoulder with a lopsided smile.

Jason and I went to the living room to eat the cake. As I got ready to cut the first piece, he realized we didn't have any ice cream. I wasn't tripping, but he was set on getting some. He slipped on his jacket and walked to the corner store. While he was gone, I took a quick shower. Water ran down my head as I closed my eyes, but I immediately popped them open when I heard the door squeak. I stuck my head out the shower to see my mother twirling the ends of her sandy blond hair wearing a silk night gown that was falling off her frail body. Fuck! I thought I locked the door. I grabbed my towel from off the shower rod and wrapped it around my waist to cover my dick.

"Can I get some privacy?"

"It's nothing I haven't seen before baby," she gave a sinister smile.

I shook my head and stepped out the shower disregarding her inappropriate looks as she lustfully raked her eyes down my body. As I walked past her to reach for the doorknob, she gripped the hems of my towel trying to pull it off. With a scowl penetrating my face, I pushed her hard on the floor. She leaped up with a crazed look in her eyes and began hitting me on my back, calling me all types of sissy bitches.

"Why am I a sissy bitch? Because I won't fuck you? That shit ain't normal. You're my mother!" I yelled.

"Aww shut up you little punk. I know who the fuck I am. I got the stretch marks to prove it," she rolled her eyes, "I got needs and you as my son are obligated to take care of them until I find a man who could. Don't you love me and want to keep me happy?"

"I ain't having sex with you!" I yelled.

"You're gonna do what the hell I tell you to do or I am tossing your ungrateful ass out my place. I ain't gonna have two hard dicks in here not paying any bills and not giving me no dick. Hell no."

"Woman you're sick," I spoke through my gritted teeth.

As a young boy, my mother had made me do things to her body that a son shouldn't have. It really messed me up. She was sick in the head for real. Her betrayal had me questioning if I would ever be able to properly love a woman. Sometimes, I wondered if she did the same things to my brother because he hated her just as much as I did. I couldn't wait to get the fuck away from her for good.

"Ssssh, you bastards aren't no prize! Neither was ya'll black ass daddy!" she yelled.

The sound of the front door slamming silenced our argument as Jason strolled in with a rageful look in his eyes carrying a black plastic bag. He immediately stood in front me with his feet planted firmly on the floor and my shaking body immediately relaxed. I swallowed hard looking at the intense stare down between the two of them. Neither one of them uttered a word. When my mother pulled out a cigarette to light up, the hairs on the back of my neck stood up. It had been a long time since she burned us, but the memory was still engrained in my memory. I could tell from the way Jason's jaws locked up; he was ready to snap. She called herself being funny and walked up to him to blow smoke rings in his face. That's when Jason unexpectedly gripped her neck. Tighter and tighter, he squeezed, and I could see her chest rising as she struggled to breathe.

Her pale face began to turn blue and I placed my hand on his shoulder so he could stop. Jason had a bright future in front of him and I didn't want him to waste it by going to prison for strangling our mother to death. He released his grip and tossed her to the floor like a sack of potatoes.

"Get the fuck out my house!" she struggled to catch her breath.

"This place belongs to section- 8 you white bitch, so it ain't your house. I suggest you not try that shit again or you won't be so lucky next time," Jason threatened, "Maurice, let's go finish celebrating your birthday."

I followed behind Jason as I stared at my mother who remained on the floor sobbing. We went to our bedroom and sat on the floor staring deeply at the wall.

"How long has mom been messing with you Maurice? Please don't lie to me."

"Since I was nine. It started out with her kissing me, rubbing on my private area but then she started wanting me to do other things like rubbing on her. I didn't want to, but she told me she would beat you if I didn't. I didn't want her to hurt you, so I did it, but I didn't like it," I sighed.

"That nasty bitch told me the same thing and she still ended up messing with you. I'm sorry she hurt you man, but I promise she will never do that shit again," his voice cracked.

Later on that night, Jason left out and came back with my mother's drugs after she begged him to go meet her dealer. I noticed before he gave it to her, he slipped in the kitchen. When he tossed her the little baggie, her eyes lit up. She began setting up her spoon, and other things she needed to get high. I went to the bedroom, while Jason went to the bathroom. Then, I heard a loud thud and got up to check out the noise. My heart began beating wildly in my chest seeing my mother sprawled out on the floor with black stuff oozing from her mouth. With haste, I ran to bathroom and began banging on the door to get Jason. He opened it looking at me with his eyebrows knitted together.

"We got to call 911. I think Sarah is overdosing," I wiped the sweat off my face.

"I ain't calling shit. She deserves to die for what she did to us. Nasty bitch," Jason could care less, "I should've thought of this a long time ago."

"Jason, what did you do?"

He heavily sighed before looking at me with tears in his eyes, "I did what I had to do to protect us. I put something in her drugs to kill her. She is no longer able to hurt you ever again. You don't hate me, do you?"

"No, I can never hate you. I love you bro."

"And I love you too and nobody is gonna come between that," he pulled me into a hug.

We waited for a while to call the police and told them she had overdosed on heroin.

I woke up from my sleep covered in sweat and sat up on my bed. Every time on my birthday, I had the same dream. That night, it was either saving a woman's life who tormented us or spare my brother who protected me. I chose to be my brother's keeper. In the end, Jason went on to be a successful doctor, but the demons of his past always came back to haunt him. From childhood to adulthood, he remained in tremendous pain. I guess suicide was the only way he could find peace. I just wish he would of reached out to me before making his final decision.

* * *

I was a man of my word and allowed that nigga Martell some more time to get my money. It was finally time to collect the rest. He walked into my office with his pants sagging, wearing a fake rope chain that was turning green. Rich stood up to pat him down before allowing him to take a seat in front of my desk. Scowling my face, I extended my hand out without even acknowledging him, and he placed the knot of cash in my hand. Removing the dirty rubber band, I began to count it to make sure it was all there before ripping all of it into shreds. Then I tossed it into his face and stood up from my chair. It was never about getting the money back. Two thousand wasn't shit, especially when I was sitting on millions. I just didn't like to be played with. I took my business seriously.

"I want to know why did it feel like I was chasing you when you owed me money. The only reason why I let you get down with me because you are Winter's cousin, and she vouched for you. I don't feel you're tough enough for this business. It ain't got anything to do with you liking to put your dick into another nigga's ass. I been knowing you were a sissy. You can't be trusted," I angrily spoke and punched him in his face.

"Fuck! Look, Maino. I didn't mean no harm. I promise this won't happen again. You will get your money immediately without any problems," he assured me.

"Next time? Nigga, it ain't no next time. This is your only time. We are done doing business. This meeting right here is to figure out if you are gonna continue to breathe or not." I removed my gun from my pants and pointed it at his head.

I watched a sheen of sweat roll off his eyebrows, and he dropped his head, releasing a deep breath. Cocking back my gun, I placed the barrel at his sweaty temple. As he teared up, there was a knock on the door. I motioned my head to Rich to answer it. The sound of my oldest daughter's voice caught me by surprise. I quickly went to hide my gun inside one of the drawers of my desk. A smiling Mira pushed through the door holding her baby sister, Nova's, hand as Ace walked behind them cradling my granddaughter in a blanket. They were all taking me out to dinner to celebrate my birthday, but they weren't supposed to be there. I was expecting them later than the time they arrived. When I saw Nova rush to give her cousin, Martell, a hug, I saw the relief on that nigga's face.

"Hi, Tell. You want to see my baby?" she showed him a toy doll.

"Sure, let me see it, little cuz." He stood up like everything was straight.

"Sit your ass down!" I yelled.

"Daddy, did I do something wrong?" Nova's little lip quivered.

I prided myself on never letting my kids see me angry. Dropping my scowl, I immediately felt bad for getting out of character and scooped my princess into my arms. She wrapped her tiny arms around my shoulders to snuggle me closely before I kissed her cheek.

"I wasn't yelling at you or anybody else. Daddy sometimes talks too loud when he gets excited. You ready to go eat?" I kissed her cheek again.

"Yes, daddy. I want cake," she giggled.

"Cake it is, sweetheart. Ace, can you do me a favor and take them outside? We got to finish up this meeting." He nodded his head.

"No problem," Ace agreed.

"Dad, hurry up. We're ready to go," Mira complained.

"One minute, I promise."

The door closed and I punched Martell directly in his mouth. His lips immediately swelled up. Then I wrapped my hands around his neck, choking him. Slowly, his eyes began rolling to the back of his head. I released my grip, and he gasped loudly for air with his chest weaving.

"You're no longer working for me. The only reason why you're still breathing is because of Nova. She actually loves you, but I don't give a fuck about you. Just know, your life was only spared because of that. If you see me coming, you better turn the other direction. Now get the fuck!"

He leaped up so fast, knocking the chair on the floor, and bolted out my office without looking back at me. It was time to get out of business mode to focus on being with my family.

They escorted us to a private dining room when we arrived at the restaurant. They had the chef prepare me her best dishes. Spread across the table were Porterhouse steaks, lobster, gumbo, asparagus, and rosemary potatoes. She even fried little dinosaur nuggets for Nova. She kept stuffing them into her mouth like somebody was going to take them. I playfully snuck a nugget off her plate, and she frowned her face.

"Daddy, don't you take food off my plate. That's rude. No, thank you." She shook her tiny finger.

"I can't have one, baby girl? You hurt my feelings." I laid my hand on my chest.

"Don't be sad. You can have one," she offered with a smile.

"What about me?" Ace chimed in with a smirk.

"Big brother, you can have one but my niecey can't because she is a baby. She only can drink milk."

"Oh really? You gonna forget about me? Your big sister? I know you're not, miss thang," Mira teased with a smile.

"Oh, no, silly. I can't forget about you, Mira bear. Here." She fed her sister a nugget.

Ace had to go to the bathroom and handed me my granddaughter. I cradled her in my arms as she looked up at me with widened eyes. She slightly smiled when I touched her little cheek. I loved being a paw paw.

"What's up, lil mama? I bet you're gonna be a doctor too." She laughed like she knew what I was talking about.

When Ace returned back to the table, the chef brought out a chocolate cake for dessert. As I was looking down at my phone to see the time, Mira smashed a piece in my face and started cracking up, holding her stomach.

"I got you back, dad for all those years you did it to me." Mira was hyped.

"You got me." I wiped some of the icing off my face.

"So, this is a tradition, huh? I see now. I got to get in on this too." Ace smiled.

I felt bad about missing Ace's birthdays but vowed never to do it anymore. As he was still laughing with his sisters, I grabbed a small piece of cake and shoved it into his face.

"You ain't got to wait until next year. I got you today," I laughed.

We finished eating dessert and went back to my place. Winter was outside sitting inside her car. My jaws locked, and I felt tension immediately in my neck. She climbed out holding balloons with a smile. Everyone else went inside. When she tried to give me a kiss on my lips, I turned my head.

"What are you doing here?" I raked my hands down my face.

"I wanted to come wish you a happy birthday, baby. Didn't you get my text message?"

"Yeah, and I erased it. If it ain't got anything to do with our daughter, we don't need to talk."

I left her standing outside looking stupid. I tossed my cellphone on the table and finished kicking it with my kids and my granddaughter. We played a few games while eating snacks. My cellphone began vibrating. It was a text message from Morgan.

Morgan: *Mango head, I thought we were cool. Why didn't you tell me it was your birthday? I had to find out in the streets. What did you do today? I hope you got treated like a king.*

Me: *My kids took me to dinner and now we just chilling.*

Morgan: *That's all? You ain't do anything adventurous? We are going to have to change that, big head. Do you have any plans tomorrow?*

Me: *I can clear my schedule. What did you have in mind?*

Morgan: *You will see. Just wear something comfortable but don't put on sweatpants. I don't want to be looking at your dick print all day.*

Me: *I can't help that my dick big. You need to do your best and not look at it.*

Morgan: *Duh, that's why I said don't be wearing those trap-a-bitch sweatpants. I don't know what I am gonna do. Now continue celebrating with your kids, and I will see you tomorrow.*

Me: *You want me to pick you up or you're driving?*

Morgan: *You can pick me up. I don't feel like driving.*

I put my phone down to focus on the movie and saw Mira smirking at me curiously. She didn't ask me any questions, but every time I was texting on my phone, she kept peering over my shoulders trying to see the name on my screen. We stayed up for another two hours until Ace needed to get Ava home. I walked them to their ride and waited for him to strap my grandbaby in her car seat, who was looking exhausted. We pulled each other in a hug before he got in and left. My birthday was complete. I finally had all my kids together.

* * *

As I pulled up to Morgan's building, my music was blasting, and my whip smelled like a weed dispensary. I sprayed some lavender scent to decrease the smell before stepping out my driver's seat. Morgan strutted down the steps wearing a black shirt and leggings with some Jordan's. We embraced in a tight hug, and then I opened up her door. She sunk into the leather seat putting her big bag on her lap. I didn't know what came over me and just leaned down to give her a long kiss. When I lifted my head, she unexpectedly gripped hold of my shirt and snuck another kiss. Then, she shifted her eyes to my sweatpants. I watched as she glided her tongue across her lips.

"Didn't I tell you not to wear those trap-a-bitch pants? I can already see that big ass dick coming to play peak-a-boo." Morgan grinned.

"I can't help that I'm blessed. Just have some self-control and stop looking." I smirked.

"That's the problem. I don't have any self-control. I'm the dick police." She grabbed my shit.

Morgan didn't care what the hell came out of her mouth. Her carefree personality was one of the reasons why I was attracted to her. I shut the passenger door walking around to get in my ride. After I got settled and put on my seatbelt, she told me we were going to a gun range, and she put the address in my GPS system. I had never been to one before. I learned how to shoot in the streets.

"Do you even know how to shoot a gun?" I asked Morgan as she put some lipstick on her lips.

"No, but I was hoping you were going to help me. I mean, you are a drug dealer. I assume that's a part of the business to know how to shoot." She placed her hand on my knee.

"It is, but I ain't trying to get shot fucking with you," I laughed.

"Oh, shut up. This gives you an opportunity to put your dick on my ass and to be up on me." She smiled.

"I rather be inside you," I confessed.

"Lord, please help me," she fanned herself.

At the gun range, we were given waiver forms and went over safety rules before handing us ear covers along with protective eye gear. I cocked the gun back as Morgan stood a few feet behind me to watch me shoot the silhouette target. Aiming for the head, I squeezed the trigger. Then, I went for the chest hitting it without any issue. The first time I ever shot a gun, I killed some nigga that I had beef with from my old neighborhood. I was sixteen. By the time I was twenty-five, I couldn't keep up with my body count. Placing the gun on safety, I turned around to look at Morgan, and she was nodding her head in approval.

"Come here so I can help you shoot," she stood in front of me, and I taught her how to carefully hold a gun, "Relax, Morg. Let me guide you. You do trust me, don't you?"

"I do," she breathed heavily.

"That's what I like to hear, baby." I kissed the back of her neck.

I instructed Morgan to put her index finger on the trigger and squeeze. She hit the target several times in the chest with my assistance. There was a sense of pride looking into her eyes.

"Nobody better mess with me or I will bust a cap in their ass." She was excited.

"Morg, you crazy, girl. Ain't nobody in their right mind would give you a gun," I laughed.

We left the gun range, and Morgan invited me back to her spot for some lunch. She prepared lasagna. My stomach was stuffed sitting on the couch as she laid in my arms watching television. One of my jump-offs began blowing me up. She did her best to ignore my ringing phone, but she could no longer keep quiet.

"If you got somewhere to be, you could leave." She seemed a little upset.

"Damn. You are growing sick of me already and trying to put me out." I rubbed the waves in my head.

"No, but apparently, one of your hoes wants to get your attention. I was gonna let you bounce." She pursed her lips.

"They might want mines, but I want yours." I turned off my phone, pulled her feet on my lap, and massaged them.

* * *

I stepped through the metal detector of the prison and then grabbed my identification card from the female correctional officer. There were a couple of seats in the waiting area, but I chose to lean against the wall. I glanced around, looking at the people from different ages and ethnicities eagerly waiting to visit their loved ones. A little boy who looked to be around eight sat next to his mother. I couldn't imagine my children having to visit me behind prison walls. I worked tirelessly to stay under the radar while making my money. I never wanted to get cased up and taken away from my kids' lives. Leaving them in the world to fend for themselves wasn't an option. When it was my time to be taken back to see my partner, J-Rock, I got escorted to a metal table next to a vending machine where he was already sitting, eating on some Skittles.

"Long time no see nigga. How you been, man?" J-Rock smiled and pulled me into a dap hug.

"I can't call it. Grinding and taking care of the family."

"No doubt. I 'preciate you are looking out for my mom dukes while I'm behind these walls."

"You ain't got to thank me. We supposed to look out for each other."

"What's been up? How is business?" he asked.

"Good," I kept it short.

J-Rock looked over his shoulders to make sure nobody wasn't ear hustling before leaning into to talk to me about doing business with his cellmates' brother, who was from Mexico. The dude was looking to buy product because his former connect had people overdosing left and right from his product. It was drawing attention and putting their organization at risk. I wasn't feeling the idea because we didn't know them, but I let J-Rock speak without interrupting. When he finished his pitch, I remained silent, rubbing my beard.

"I'm telling you, man. These Migos got money and they ready to spend it with us. I'm talking millions on top of what you're making now. If you're down, I can have my cellmate hit up his brother so we can setup the meeting. What you think? I'm trying to get paid." He was hyped.

"There isn't a need to make the call because I ain't doing business with him. You said it yourself. Their organization is being looked at because of the dead bodies. For all I know, FED's can be surveilling them right now to build a case. I can't take that risk regardless of how good the money is, neither can you."

"Nigga, I didn't ask you for your permission. I'm telling you what we are doing when I get out from behind these walls." His nostrils flared.

"You ain't doing a mothafuckin' thing without my permission. You might have started the business, but I built it. I wasn't just keeping your throne warm, nigga. I was taking over and making moves. I make so much money even when I am sleeping. I won't allow a bad deal to ruin that or take away my freedom."

"It's like that, huh? Nigga been locked down ten years, and you don't think I know how to conduct business. I taught you the game."

"I took it to the next level. You wasn't running nothing from in here out there. Everything that you know that's going on in the streets, is because of me, nigga! I'ma give you a pass, J, but it ain't your world no more." I walked out the visitor's hall.

Chapter Twelve
MORGAN REID

The meetings at my law firm were boring as hell. I was on my fifth cup of coffee just to stay awake. It was impossible to focus when my boss, Mr. Carmichael's, voice was flat and boring without any excitement. On top of that, he took forever getting to the point. I wanted to snatch his presentation clicker from his hand and shove it up his white ass. When my head began to drop, my colleague, Sandy, nudged me on the arm. I popped my eyes open to see her holding a coffee mug, while frowning. We were the only two black people at the office, but I couldn't stand that heffa. She was always trying to kiss up to the white folks and stayed trying to marginalize herself from anything black with her Uncle Tom ass. Anytime she was given cases to represent anybody of color, she refused or automatically assumed they were guilty. If you asked me, she should've been lucky she had an opportunity to get any clients. I saw the heffa's portfolio and wasn't impressed. She graduated at the bottom of her law school and worked on mediocre cases before taking a position at Carmichael's firm. The only reason why she got hired was because she was fuckin' our boss's son, who was a fuck up.

"I suggest you refrain from watching BET all night if you can't stay up and do your job." She pursed her lips.

"If you don't want me to go upside your head, you better watch those elbows," I spoke through my gritted teeth.

"Excuse me?" she clutched her imaginary pearls like she was offended.

"You heard me loud and clear, Uncle Tom. You need to worry about sucking that little pink dick instead of worrying about what shows I'm watching."

I worked hard to get in my position, not fucking my way up the cooperate ladder.

She hiked her nose at me without uttering another word and focused her attention back on our boss. As for me, I pulled out my cellphone and discreetly began texting Maino under the conference table about my boring meeting. He immediately got back to me, sending a few laughing emoji's.

Me: *Come save me. I don't think I am going to last. I have to be in this boring meeting another hour, and then I have to work with this Uncle Tom heffa on a new case. I don't feel like being at work. I knew I should've called the hell out. Damn.*

Maino: *What are you going to do if I help you get out of work?*

Me: *Anything you want except sucking your dick.*

Maino: *You're funny as hell, girl. Do you have a secretary or personal assistant?*

Me: *Yes, it's Lovely, but she isn't back from maternity leave, so they got this chick named Alexis. Why?*

Maino: *Don't worry about it. Just send me the contact information. Be prepared to put on a show.*

I smiled, shaking my head, and placed my phone on the table before picking up my pen to jot down some notes on my notepad. Five minutes later, my secretary knocked on the door and interrupted our meeting to tell me it was a family emergency. My niece, Tinka, was in the hospital. I didn't have a damn niece, but I went along with it. My boss gave me a sympathetic expression before giving me permission to leave. I leaped from my seat and frantically gathered my stuff off the table, bolting out the conference room being dramatic.

When I entered my office, I grabbed my suitcase, tossed a few files in, and rushed out. The elevator was going downstairs, so I jumped on with a few people. I kept my worried facial expression until I pulled out my assigned parking space. Then, I began pumping my fist in the air before calling Maino on my phone.

"Yo, what's good?" his deep baritone voice filled my car.

"I'm out of work. Thank goodness." I was hyped and began beeping my horn.

"Good to know. Now, you can come kick it with me."

"I might can find some time with you after I am done at the nail salon."

I badly wanted to spend time with Maino, but I damn sure didn't need him thinking I was sprung. Cocky men like him loved to use that to their advantage if they knew a woman was falling for them. As much as I hated to admit, ya girl was falling head over heels for him. For some reason, I couldn't leave him alone. I tried several times to put him on the block list, but I would take him off. His attention fed my soul.

"Morg, you ain't going to use me to get out of work and not kick it. After you come from getting your feet done, I am going to scoop you up from your place. You can go with me to get a tattoo, and then we can figure out what to do next."

"I always wanted to get some ink, but I'm scared. Does it hurt?"

"The pain is tolerable. To me, it feels like a pinch." He was nonchalant.

"Please. Your entire body is covered in ink, so of course you're gonna say it doesn't hurt." I wasn't convinced.

"My cousin owns a shop and she does all my ink. She is a beast. How about you come see me get mine done? If you like her work, she can do yours too."

Tattoos were sexy, and people used them as a way to express themselves creatively. I had been contemplating about getting me one, but I was petrified of needles. My fear of them began as a child when my mother had me shoot her junkie friend with dope. I damn near killed the man by injecting too much into his body. One of the scariest moments of my life was watching him slumped over on our worn-out couch with foam coming from his mouth. It still got me emotionally worked up thinking about it. Nonetheless, I was ready to put my fears to the side and get me my first tattoo.

"Fine, I will do it, but you got to hold my hand."

"I won't let go, Morg," he agreed.

After getting my pedicure, I went home to change into some relaxing clothes and shoes. With my hair blowing in the wind, I stepped out my building, and Maino was sitting in his truck. As I got ready to pull the door handle, he immediately leaped out to assist me. He was truly a gentleman despite his street reputation. We drove to the tattoo parlor, and his huge hand remained comfortably on my thigh, making me blush. I noticed he had the initials, JP, in cursive tattooed on his hand. It had to be new because it wasn't there at first.

"Are those your brother's initials?" I rubbed my fingers on top of the letters.

"Yeah. I just got it done," he momentarily glanced at me before facing back at the road.

Although Jason committed suicide over a year ago, it still felt fresh. I truly felt bad that he felt he no longer could live. Eva told me the night he killed himself, he tried to win her back.

"I'm sorry."

"For what, Morg?" his forehead scrunched up.

"That you had to bury your brother. I know that has to be difficult. I mean, he did hurt my best friend, but I didn't want him to die."

"It hurts. He was my big brother. My protector."

"Were you close when you were kids?"

"Yeah, you couldn't see me without seeing him. He was truly my keeper, but I wish I could've been his. And before you say it, I couldn't save him. It still won't stop me from feeling guilty."

"I understand." I rubbed his leg for support.

My heart truly ached for Maino. I didn't want to make our time together sad and switched the subject to sports. We began talking about the shitty ass Washington Football Team and my Baltimore Ravens. He then told me to open his glove compartment, and there were a couple of tickets to their game in the luxury skybox at FedEx Field. I placed them against my chest and began screaming with excitement about attending the game until he busted my bubble.

"Those ain't for you. I'm taking Ace."

"Why the hell did you get my hopes up, fool? I already had my outfit in my head." I kissed my teeth.

"I didn't, sweetheart. You just assumed and I let you," he chuckled.

"Kiss my black ass." I folded my arms against my chest with a frown.

"I plan to one day, Ms. Reid," he chuckled, "Do you think he's gonna like them?"

"Hell yeah, I do. You are sure his geeky ass like football? I can go in his place."

"That's not nice to talk about your future stepson," he chuckled.

"Whatever. I am so pissed right now." I pouted.

"Don't be. The tickets are for us. We are going to the game tomorrow." He gave me a lopsided grin.

"For real?"

"Yeah, baby. For real."

"Hell yessssssss." I was hyped and pumped my fist.

We pulled into the parking lot and got out his truck. Maino grabbed my hand as we walked inside the tattoo parlor. A female with long, beautiful healthy locs approached us smirking. She pulled Maino into a friendly hug before setting her sights on me with a smirk.

"Big cuz, who this be?" the female probed.

"His girlfriend Morgan," I blurted out and she shook my hand.

"Girlfriend, it's nice to meet you. My name is Bria."

"My girl is trying to get some work done. Being that you're the best, I brought her here to get inked up." Maino placed his hand on my back.

"You already know my tattoos are the shit, cuzzo. Let me hook y'all up." She smiled and walked around the counter.

I leaned up against the counter, flipping through the pages of the portfolio designs, and Maino came behind me. He then wrapped his arms around my waist before kissing the nape of my neck. A relaxed smile pulled on my lips, and I kept on looking at the selections. Nothing really caught my attention, so I decided to get cat paws. The design was dedicated to my fur baby, Tink, who came in my life during my darkest time.

"What are you getting? I think for your first tat it should be small just in case the pain is too intense." He stared at me with his hooded eyes.

"Cat paws on my boobs to represent my baby." I pointed to the top of my breast where I planned to put them.

"Cat paws? You really about to put something on your skin for that stinky ass furball." He rubbed the back of his neck in disbelief.

"Don't talk about my baby Tink. He is my child. It was either that or a big black dick." I pursed my lips.

Maino dropped his head laughing and then pulled me close to his body. I noticed he had been very touchy. However, that didn't bother me. My love language was physical touch. We followed his cousin to a well-lighted room where black and white artwork hung on the wall. Some were from clients who had taken pictures of the end results. I thought it was cool seeing how happy people were with their tattoos. While I took a closer look at the art displayed on the wall, Bria prepped her materials for our tattoos. When she was set up at her station, Maino stripped off his Fendi sweater and tossed it at me with a laugh. Then, he sat down on the leather seat intently looking at me. The ink gun pierced his bicep, and he didn't even react to the pain.

When it was my turn to get my ink, I felt a tightness in my throat, and sweat beads began emerging on my forehead. While I sat down, I took deep breaths, drawing in and out as Maino held my hand. Just like a big baby, I began sobbing the moment the gun touched my skin. I managed to calm down as Maino talked to me and rubbed my hair. The cat paws on my breasts were beautiful as I proudly looked at the mirror. The pain was worth it. My paws were covered up before I was given instructions on how to keep it healthy.

After we left the tattoo shop with our fresh ink, we grabbed some food and went to my condo. Maino refused to try the sushi and kept frowning his face when I tried to feed him with the chopsticks. He was acting like a little baby.

"You need to open your mind and try something new. It's more to good food than fried chicken and swine." I pinched his cheek, and he shook his head with a smile.

"I don't want this shit. It ain't even done. You're gonna mess around and catch food poisoning," he fussed.

I popped a piece of sushi into my mouth and began dancing in my seat. He just took out his phone while I ate to watch some sports highlights. I felt kind of bad for him watching me and offered to order him something from one of the food apps.

"I don't want any of that food. My mouth is craving a taste of your pussy. Open up and come feed me." He licked his lips.

I found myself laying on my kitchen table with my legs spread open as he sat in a chair indulging on my pussy. He kept dipping his index finger into my wet hole while he latched on my clit and jerked his big thick dick. Back-to-back, I climaxed into his mouth. I was sexually and ready to get fucked. Yet, he wouldn't touch me with his dick. He just pleasured me using his tongue until my body was weak and I could no longer cum. As my underwear were hanging off my left ankle, and my chest was beating rapidly, Maino lowered his lips to mine, giving me a taste of my natural scent. Our kiss was interrupted when my cell phone began ringing. I hopped up off the table and went to answer it. The sound of my uncle crying sent me on high alert. He began telling me how his boyfriend smacked him because he was in a bad mood after he got fired by Maino.

My nostrils flared and I began pacing the floor as I allowed him to vent until he calmed down. Even though I didn't want to stop hanging with Maino, I made an excuse about having to meet one of my clients that was in a dire situation. He totally understood and I walked him to his truck. He gently placed a kiss on my temple. That's when I cuffed both sides of his cheeks, leaving him with a long kiss.

"I want to see you again. Let's have dinner tonight." He kissed the crook of my neck, and I felt my breathing increase as my heart rate sped up.

"Seven thirty works for me. Leave your boxers at home too," I joked.

"Yo, you are tripping. I ain't gonna be air balling out this bitch."

"Why not? I might get the urge to suck your dick on the go."

"You crazy, Morg," he laughed. "How about you leave your underwear off so I can have access to my dessert?" he flirted and gripped my ass.

I kissed Maino one last time, and he climbed in his truck to drive off. The adrenaline was pumping through my body as I pressed the numbers on the keypad to my unit door. Stripping out my clothes, I took a shower and put on some loose workout gear. Then, I grabbed my taser putting it in my tote bag. With haste, I made my way to my truck and pulled out of my parking garage. When I pulled up to my uncle's house, I grabbed my purse from my back seat. Banging loudly on the door, Martell opened it frowning. Before he knew what hit him, I pulled my taser, sending volts up to his body, making him repeatedly shake. Then, I gripped hold of his balls, squeezing them while I bit down on my teeth. He grunted in agony with his eyes tightly shut. That's when my uncle rushed towards us and started shouting with tears rolling down his cheeks to release his man.

"Morgan, stop. You're going to break his balls," he was worried.

"That's my plan." I squeezed tighter.

"Please, stop it, niece," he begged.

Sighing, I released my death grip off Martell's balls before striking him in the face as hard as I could using my taser. He fell backwards on the floor, and I hovered over top of him. My uncle had the audacity to rush to his side and held him closely, giving me a dirty look when he had a knot the size of an egg on top of his forehead.

"I called you to confide. Not for you to come fight my man." He snaked his neck.

"Got damn it! Well, stop calling me then because I don't have all my screws. I no longer want to hear about your no-good man. He ain't shit and isn't going to change. You're too stupid to see it anyway." I was angry.

"Everyone isn't strong like you. I am glad you got out your situation with Shannon, but nobody wants to be old and alone like you," Courtney said.

"Don't you dare bring that nigga up again. Call me when you get a clue." I slammed the door.

My uncle could take that nigga back if he wanted, but Martell was going to know not to put his hands on him again. If he did, I might just ask Maino to send that down low, non-hustling nigga to the upper room.

Chapter Thirteen

MAURICE "MAINO" PIERCE

Sprawled out on my bed, my cellphone began to vibrate loudly on my nightstand. I slowly opened my eyes, answered the phone, and placed it against my ear. Layla's muffled sobs had me on high alert as I sat up to turn on my lamp.

"What's going on?" I panicked.

"You need to get to GW hospital. Mira was in a car accident," she sobbed.

My phone immediately slipped out my hand hearing that my baby girl was in a car accident and was taken to the hospital. Without a second thought, I hopped up from my bed, rushing into my walk-in closet. I tossed on some clothes and left out the front door holding my key fob. Running every red light, I made it to the hospital in no time. I illegally parked my Benz in front of the Emergency Room entrance and bolted through the automatic doors with my heart wildly beating in my chest.

Anxiously glancing around the waiting area, I spotted Layla wearing a robe, pacing the floor with tears rolling down her face. Her husband was there too, sitting on a chair somberly holding his head. I rushed over to Layla, and she collapsed in my arms, weeping. While holding her tight, she explained how she let Mira use her new car to go with her friends to a party.

"The family of Mira Pierce?" the doctor came out with a somber look on his face.

"How is my daughter, Doc? Is she going to be okay?" I was worried out my mind.

"I'm sorry. We lost Mira five minutes ago." The doc gave us the worst news a parent could ever hear.

Releasing a gut-wrenching sob, Layla dropped down to the floor on her knees, while her husband held her in his arms to console her.

"Fuck you mean! She ain't dead! I was just with her." I looked at the doctor with my teeth baring and eyes widened.

"Sir, we did all we could. I'm sorry." The doctor dropped his head, sighing.

I blacked out and gripped hold of the doctor's neck. I shook him like he was the person who took her life. Six security guards had to restrain me as I tried to run to find which room my daughter was in.

"Mira! Mira! Daddy is here. NOOOO!" I sobbed.

Police were called to the hospital after my emotional breakdown, but they had sympathy when they found out I lost my child. The female officer removed my handcuffs from my wrists and demanded that I was able to see my daughter. Reluctantly, the medical staff agreed, and I was escorted to the room that my baby girl was in. My baby mama, Layla, refused to see our baby girl and remained outside the door sobbing. The sharp pain I was feeling in my heart was unbearable as I saw Mira's lifeless body lying on the bed with a gigantic gash in the center of her forehead. My lips quivered, as I softly rubbed her hair and kissed her cheek. As tears glided down my cheeks, I scooped her into my arms and rocked her like a baby.

"Please forgive daddy for not protecting you," my voice cracked.

Honestly, I didn't remember how I made it home after staying with Mira's body because I was just so out of it. I tossed my key and just sat on my couch staring at the wall crying.

A couple hours later, I heard my doorbell, but I didn't answer. When my phone began ringing, I still didn't move. The person who was trying to get in contact with me was relentless. I began hearing banging on my front door. That shit just had me full of rage. Removing the liquor bottle from my lips, I slammed it on the floor, stomping heavily to the door. I snatched it open to see Morgan wearing a Ravens jersey. My mind was so fucked up I forgot about the game we were supposed to attend.

"Hey, big head. Don't tell me you forgot about going to the game with me." She smiled.

"We ain't going to the game today."

"Why, is everything okay?" she looked concerned.

"I just want to be alone. Now leave," my voice cracked.

I did my best to hold back my tears, not wanting to show my weakness, but they began to roll down my cheeks. My world had been shattered, and it would never be the same. I couldn't believe I was gonna bury my child. My Mira bear.

"Maino, please tell me what's wrong? Is there anything I can do to help? I can call Ace if you prefer him to help. I just don't feel comfortable leaving you like this alone." She was panicked.

"Ain't shit you can do to help. Can you bring my dead daughter back? I want to be alone. I lost my baby. My daughter is dead. She ain't never coming back." I broke down with my hands over my face.

Reality had sunken into my head, how I would have to bury my daughter causing me to snap. I pulled down the flat screen off the wall mount, slamming it on the floor, broke my vases by slamming them on the floor, and flipped over my glass coffee table. My chest weaved slowly as tears rolled down my cheek. Morgan hesitantly approached me with glossy eyes before placing the palm of her hand on my cheek. She then pulled me in a hug, and I released a breath I didn't even know I was holding. As much as I wanted her to leave so I could mourn, a part of me also wanted her to stay. She gently grabbed my hand, encircling her fingers into mine, and walked me to the couch. Sighing heavily, I plopped down on the cushion as she disappeared into my kitchen. She came back with a club sandwich on a plate and a bottle of water. I didn't have an appetite.

"I am not hungry." I frowned when she tried to put the sandwich next to my mouth.

"Just take a bite please. You won't have any energy if you don't put something in your system." She was worried.

"How many times I have to tell you I ain't hungry!" I yelled, and she jumped.

"Okay, I won't press you," she didn't put up a fight and placed the plate on the arm of the couch, "Have you told Ace?"

"No," I sighed.

"Do you want me to call him?"

"I don't need anybody to help me with my own son. How about you just leave?"

I left Morgan sitting on the couch and went to take a shower. As the water ran down my head, I silently sobbed with my eyes shut. My body softly shook when the breeze hit it. I opened my eyes seeing Morgan stepping into the shower butt naked. She raised her hands up, surrendering as I shot her a dirty look. I told her to leave, but she was still there in my personal space. I got ready to open the sliding door and she gripped my arm. She just held me close while I sobbed with my arms wrapped around her body.

"Morg, I would do anything to trade places with my daughter to spare her life."

"I know, Maino. I know," she sobbed too.

I had taken many lives and saw many dead bodies. However, seeing my baby girl dead, hit differently. I didn't how I was going to make it.

Chapter Fourteen
MORGAN REID

I was at my law firm sitting in the conference room jotting down notes after my boss begged me to represent his son, who was facing vehicular homicide charges. He was too emotional to take on the case, so he needed the best and that was me. My track record for winning cases was in the ninety-five percentile. I wasn't afraid to go above and beyond to get the job done.

"Mr. Carmichael, I can assure you that your son's case is in good hands. If I can make a suggestion, I think he should go to some type of rehab facility. It's difficult to conquer addiction alone, and it might show the jurors that he's being accountable for his actions," I suggested.

"My son is no addict. He occasionally likes to drink and had far too many that night. I feel bad for all parties involved, but I will do anything to make sure my son doesn't go to jail," his voice cracked, and his eyes became watery.

Mr. Carmichael was in denial about his son's drinking problem. He had several DUI's and got his license suspended because of it. Firmly shaking his hand, I stood up from the wooden table and walked to my office, where Lovely was placing my coffee on my desk. My girl was a bomb ass personal assistant and kept my days so organized. I couldn't get too comfortable though. She was getting ready to graduate and get her paralegal degree, so she wasn't going to be around my office for long. Lovely was going to get her own.

"Hey, boo. You have a conference call in the next thirty minutes with one of your clients. Then, you have a lunch date with Eva's colleague, Ronell, at Fogo de Chão tomorrow at noon. I will reserve your Uber for tomorrow."

"You sure it's tomorrow? I could've sworn I had a dentist appointment." I frowned my face looking down at my electronic planner.

"Yes, it is Morgan. Don't even think about bailing out. You promised Eva you would do it. That's her colleague, and you don't want her to look like a liar, do you?" she gave me a pointed look.

I sighed heavily, picking up my coffee mug taking a sip. Those hoes were always trying to set me up on a blind date. All the men they ever hooked me up with were cornballs who couldn't fuck. I wanted a man that could stroke the kitty.

"Fine, I guess I can go out with the small dick sucka." I rolled my eyes, opening up my laptop.

"How do you know he got a small dick?" Lovely placed her hand under her chin waiting for my answer.

"I have a dickdar." I pursed my lips.

"Oh, shut up," Lovely laughed.

"For real, I do. It's a gift and a curse." I was confident.

"That's why you can't find a good man because you're always worrying about the dick."

"I sure the hell am hoe. If I'm gonna commit myself to someone for an eternity, he got to be able to fuck me. Let's be real. You wouldn't be with your husband, if he couldn't stroke."

After Lovely left my office, I opened my vanilla folder and reviewed some of the paperwork for my case. The victim that Mr. Carmichael's son killed had just graduated from high school. He was driving on the wrong side of the road and struck the front of the other driver's car. Sadly, his reckless behavior had a family mourning.

A few hours had passed by before my head began throbbing from a migraine, so I took an aspirin to relieve the tension. I got my case papers organized and went home for a nice relaxing bubble bath. As I climbed out of my Jaguar, my jaws locked, seeing my mother sitting outside of my residence smoking a cigarette. Our relationship was pretty much nonexistent. She was a pathological liar and a drug addict who only cared about getting high. That woman showed me countless times when she would leave me with her evil ass mama searching for her next high.

My mother saw me walking up to the front of the doorstep and dropped her tiny cig butt on the pavement, smashing it with her worn-out looking sneakers. She looked like she was fienin to get high. Her eyes were bloodshot red and her jaws were twitching. I couldn't give her any more money to support her habit. She reached out to give me a hug, but I put my hand up stopping her dead in her tracks. She reeked of piss, so I knew she was back living on the streets. Her honey brown skin was covered in scabs, her lips were blistered, and her gray hair was matted down.

"Morgan baby. I need a place to stay. Your uncle tossed me out because of his little ass boyfriend," she pleaded with spit building up in the corner of her mouth.

"That's not the story I got. Courtney told me you stole his boyfriend's video game."

"You know that sissy boy be lying on me, baby," she fussed.

"Don't you dare call your brother out his name. He's been there for you more than anybody, but he is sick of your crap." I was angry and honest.

"Yeah, whatever. Can I stay here for a few days? I am about to go to this rehab." I knew she was lying.

I allowed my mother to stay with me numerous of times, even after she stole some of my shit. If it wasn't nailed down, that heffa would take it to get high, but I couldn't deal with that anymore.

"No, you can't, mom. It's best you don't come around here anymore. I told you the last time, if you didn't clean yourself up, I was done with you."

My mother responded how she always did whenever she couldn't get her way. She began calling me all kinds of uppity black bitches, then tried to hock spit on me. I love my mother, and even though that shit landed on the concrete next to my feet, I forgot who she was and gripped hold of her scrawny neck. She attempted to claw at my hands, but I wasn't letting her go. She gave the most ultimate disrespect. Those were terms for 'I don't give a fuck who you are, I'm fucking yo' ass up.' She better be glad Todd was one of my good neighbors and came to pull me off. I almost choked her to death.

"Stay away from me, crackhead. I ain't got shit for you!" I was angry and went inside my condo.

* * *

The next day...

My lips pressed together with a grimace on my face. I was on a date with Ronell for only an hour and had no interest in going any further in a relationship with him. He was too in denial to notice. I felt like Vivica in that scene of 'Two Can Play That Game' when she was trying to find a date and didn't like any of them. The only reason why I entertained going out with his nerdy ass was because Eva called me shallow. I guess she was right. Don't get me wrong, I loved men who could hold stimulating conversations, but a lot of them were lacking in the dick department. I needed a Mandingo, not a Slim Jim.

"You are one fine lady, Morgan." He was trying too hard with me.

"Trust me, I know. You ain't got to tell me that. That's why you're here, right?" I pursed my lips.

All he did was chuckle, "Yea, that's right, baby. So, I guess you thinking the same thing I'm thinking then?" he smiled.

"Uhhhh, no. Actually, I need to know the time because I have a few conference calls to get on with a few clients back at my law firm." I was cutting things short.

"They can wait, girl." He placed his hand on top of mine.

"I really have to go, Ronell. Sorry, but thanks for the meal. It was very nice of you." I slid my hand from under his and walked out of the restaurant.

"Don't leave... I ain't got enough–" I heard him as I walked out the door.

He ain't have enough money, so I knew he ain't have enough dick.

I climbed in my car and called Eva to curse her ass out for setting me up on a date with George Jefferson's little brother. When I got back to the office, I got some work done for the Carmichael case. It was going to be a tough one to win, especially with my clients DUI history. As I flipped through the stapled pages, there was a loud commotion going on in the lobby. I went to see what the hell was going on and slammed into a hard upper body. Looking up, I unexpectedly saw Maino glaring at me with rage in his eyes with his jaws twitching. With my hands up, I walked backwards as he slowly followed me. That nigga looked like he was going to kill me.

"Are you representing Chase Carmichael?" his eyes looked deranged.

"Excuse me? How do you know about that, and what's that got to do with you?"

"It got everything to do with me. That white mothafucka killed my daughter. I'm not asking you, Morgan, I'm telling you, get off this case now," he spoke firmly through gritted teeth.

"I just can't abandon a case without a reason," I hesitantly explained.

"Make some shit up, but it needs to be done today." He remained firm.

I didn't know her death was connected with my case. When I tried to offer my apology, three security guards rushed in my office, holding their batons surrounding him. Maino was unfazed and began cracking his neck and balling up his fists. He hit the first guy in his mouth, and I saw a tooth fly out. Then, he headbutted the other guard unconscious. The last guard, he split his nose open. After what he did to them, I thought he was about to kill me, but he just reiterated not to take the case. He then gave me a firm stare before strolling out of my office. I knew what that meant. That nigga didn't have to say a word. I grabbed all the files pertaining to the case and put them on my boss's desk. I grew up on the streets of Baltimore. I knew when a nigga was about to take my life.

Chapter Fifteen
MAURICE "MAINO" PIERCE

As I stood on my villa patio tossing back a drink, tears welded in my eyes. Everything in my heartbeat was dedicated to my kids. Looking at Mira laying in her pink casket so young, had me mentally fucked up. I ain't never cried so damn hard in my life. Trust me, I suffered a great deal of tragedy when I lost both my parents to drug overdoses as a teenager. The pain just grew when I had to bury my older brother, Jason, after he committed suicide. However, losing a child... That shit hits differently. At the gravesite, I didn't want to leave my baby girl and stayed on top of her casket sobbing until Ace took me away. I was in so much pain and didn't even want to have a repass. A few close people in my life, got on a plane, and we flew to Maui. It was going on a week.

Ace strolled out on the patio and stood next to me holding a beer before handing it to me and placed his hand on my shoulder. My son had been very supportive, even though he was in pain too. Him and Eva went out the way to keep Layla's kids' company while she was locked up in her suite, depressed. All she did was cry and refuse to eat anything. I respected her husband Roy for staying by her side regardless of how many times she pushed him away.

"How you holdin' up, man?" Ace probed.

"I'm losing it. I'm not supposed to bury my children. Y'all are supposed to bury me," I sighed, "You alright? I know y'all was getting close." I knew he was hurting too.

"It hurts, man. Mira was a good kid. It's fucked up how these mothafuckas be driving drunk on the road and when they fuck up, they expect for someone to take things lightly. Fuck all that." Ace was angry.

He was right. That was his little sister. Some siblings who meet each other for the first time after years have passed, barely make an effort to develop a bond, but he actually cared to. They both shared an interest in medicine and planned to open a clinic together to help underprivileged people in the community.

"I know, man. I know," I sighed.

Ace had to go so he could tend to my granddaughter. After I finished my beer, I slipped my cellphone from my pocket, leaving it on the stand, and then grabbed my burner. Pulling my black hoodie on my head, I left the villa with revenge on my heart. I climbed in the waiting truck where a driver took me to a jet that was arranged by Commissioner Pratt to take me back to the states undetected. It was midnight when I touched down in the city, so I went to my house. While smoking a blunt, I hit up my worker, Dame, on my burner. He was assigned to keep tabs on the mothafucka who killed my daughter. I figured because his parents had money, they would've tried to have him relocated. I couldn't afford that.

"Where is he at?" I spoke through my gritted teeth.

"At the bar. He just got here," he revealed.

Chad Carmichael had the nerve to be still drinking after taking my child's life. White privilege at its finest. He should be behind bars, but because he wasn't, I was gonna put him in the dirt.

"Keep me posted if anything changes." I ended the call and hit up Rich.

"You en route?" I asked him.

"Be there in five."

When Rich pulled up in a moving truck, I climbed in, slipping on a pair of gloves. We headed to Chad Carmichael's house, where he lived alone. I picked the lock on his back door, and the alarm didn't sound.

It was already deactivated by the cyber security guy on my payroll. Cracking my neck, I waited in the dark living room. Two hours later, I heard movement before the door slammed. The lights flicked on as Chad staggered in drunk out of his mind. He jumped back with his hands up when he spotted me. At first, I could see the look of panic on his face, but he tried to play tough.

"Who the fuck are you?" his voice slurred.

"The last man who will see you alive," I spoke coldly.

With rage in my eyes, I hit Chad so hard and could hear his jawbone shatter. He fell back on the floor, hitting his head. I began kicking him in the face knocking him out cold. While he laid unconscious, Rich and I wrapped his body up in a carpet before taking him to the parked moving truck.

My body trembled with grief as my loud sobs reverberated throughout my chop shop. I pulled my gun from my waistband, pointing it at the drunk driver who killed my daughter. At seventeen, she was still a baby. My baby.

I had that nigga slumped over in a steel chair after beating his ass with blood leaking on his shirt. His eyes bulged open when I pressed my gun against his sweaty temple. That mothafucka had the nerve to plead for his life, yet he took my baby girl away from me. With my nostrils flared, I silenced him with three bullets to his dome. Dropping my head to the floor, I released a sigh. No words were spoken as my right-hand man, Rich, took my gun and wrapped it up in a bandana. I knew killing him wouldn't bring her back, but I wanted his family to feel the same affliction as me.

When my clean-up crew arrived to dispose of his body, I went to catch the jet back to Maui. Taking my loved ones away was to give us an alibi when the police came snooping around about Chad Carmichael's disappearance, but how can they find someone after their organs get sold on the black market for someone else to live.

* * *

A month later...

*J*jumped in the back seat of my black Benz truck, and my driver zoomed out the parking lot. He drove me to a bar down U Street because I needed a drink. The bar was crowded as always, but I found a vacant black stool next to a woman with cinnamon-brown skin who was sipping on a beer. She immediately flashed me a smile before adjusting her white top. I took that as her trying to give me a better look at her big ass titties, but I could have been wrong. However, I wasn't there to get pussy; I wanted to get drunk. Most days, I didn't want to get out of bed. Only time I got up was to get me a drink to try and numb my pain. If it wasn't for Rich taking care of the drug business, we would've crumbled.

As soon as I saw the bartender, I ordered a whiskey on the rocks. He nodded his head, flapping his white towel over his shoulder, and grabbed a bottle off the wooden shelf. He quickly poured my drink and placed the glass in front of me. Above the bar was a flat screen television casting some sports highlights. That always kept me tuned away from everything else going on around me. My glass was empty, so I motioned my hand to the bartender for another round when Morgan unexpectedly strolled in wearing a red dress that hugged her curves in all the right places. Our eyes connected, and she gave me a middle finger. She was funny like that.

Morgan reached out to me several times after my baby girl's funeral, but I wasn't in the state of mind to return any of her calls.

Morgan took a seat at the other side of the bar next to some bald-headed dude wearing a tight ass suit. They began talking and laughing immediately like they knew each other. It didn't surprise me she was into cornball brothers, but I didn't give a shit. After several rounds of small batch whiskey, the bartender cut me off. Gulping down the last drop that I had, I stood up from the stool to go to the bathroom. Then, commotion broke out on the other side of the bar. Morgan and her date were arguing.

"You really gonna run up my tab and not give me no pussy? I swear you bitches be scandalous!" the guy yelled.

"Man, please. I ain't going home with you. I saw the dick pic, baby and it wasn't anything flattering. You're not a grower or shower. Motherfucker, your ass ain't got nothing at all. The only reason why I let your tired ass take me out was for the free drinks. Now pay this tab so I can go." Morgan snaked her neck.

"Bitch, you tripping. I ain't never get any complaints from any woman."

"That itty bitty shrimp isn't pleasing shit. My cat dick is bigger than yours," Morgan laughed.

Her date leaped up from his stool and knocked it on the floor, getting all up in her face with his chest poking out like he was about to hit her. I understand his ego may have been crushed, but that wasn't manly. With haste, I rushed towards them and pushed the nigga back with aggression. I was a lot of things, but I wasn't a woman beater. And most definitely, I couldn't let my son's people get harassed in public like that. Gripping him up by the collar with my nostrils flared, I flung him over the bar counter. Then I snatched Morgan by her arm, and we left. Standing outside the bar, she immediately snatched away from me and began pointing her finger in my face like I was the one who disrespected her. She should have been thanking me for saving her narrow ass from an ass beating.

"I didn't need your help, Maino! Mind your business." She rolled her eyes.

"From what I saw, that nigga was about to fuck you up. You owe me a thank you at least." I had a smug grin on my face.

"For what? Nigga please. I ain't saying shit. You better ask your mama for an apology. Morgan Reid doesn't apologize to nobody." She pursed her lips.

"That's fucked up. You really gonna talk about my mama and you know she's dead."

"Oh, my goodness. I'm so sorry, Maino. I forgot," she was apologetic.

"You straight. I didn't like that crackhead no way." I shrugged my shoulders.

"Your mama was a crackhead too? Join the club. My mama smoked so much crack, they should've named a pipe after her thieving ass," she joked.

"Your mouth is reckless." I shook my head, chuckling.

"It sure is and who is gonna check me? Nobody, baby," she sang.

"You crazy, girl. Well, it looks like you got things under control now. I'm about to bounce." I took out my phone to call my driver.

"Where you about to go? The night is still young." She bit the edge of her lip.

"None of your damn business. You don't even like me anymore."

"True, but I ain't got shit else to do. You want to go to another bar or something? I guess I can put up with you for a few hours." She smiled.

"I get it. Your best friend is a wife and mother now, so your ass is lonely." I was hip to her game.

"So, what? Are you kicking it or what, fool?" she placed her hand on her poked-out hip.

"I'm down," I decided to entertain her. "Before we hang out, I just want to apologize to you for going MIA, when we were getting close. You didn't deserve that, but when my daughter died, I checked out mentally. Shit, I am still messed up, but I just wanted to tell you my actions didn't have anything to do with you. You're a good woman, and any man would love to have you."

"There is no need to apologize. You were in a bad place and are still dealing with the loss of your child." She grabbed my hand and squeezed it.

My driver picked us up and took us to another nightclub. There was a line wrapped around the corner with people waiting to get in, but I knew the owner, so we didn't have to wait. The bouncer rose up the red rope, and I grabbed Morgan's hand to walk in. She was looking at me like I had two heads. I wasn't trying to be romantic. Just needed her to stay close.

When I went to the nightclubs, I sat in nothing but the V.I.P areas. We went upstairs, where it was decked out in all red lights and plush leather furniture. I ordered a few bottles of Hennessy, while Morgan stood up with her hands on the rail overlooking the dance floor. She turned around, looking at me with a smirk.

"Okay, Maino. I see you how you do it. Big balling out here." She was hyped.

I just shrugged my shoulders, smirking, and popped open the first bottle of Henny, taking it to the head. Morgan was ready to turn up and started twerking with her hands in the air. I know I wasn't looking for no pussy, but she had a nigga getting rock solid. My dick was getting ready to jump out my pants. She strutted towards me and began seductively grinding her ass in my face before pulling me up by my hands to dance. Her body was doing all the talking. I matched her energy and gripped the side of her neck. I figured I shoot my shot since she was throwing it at me, so I began roughly kissing her lips. She matched pace and slipped her tongue in my mouth.

"You want to get out of here?" I kissed her neck and gripped her ass.

"Your place or mine?" Morgan smirked and grabbed my dick.

Neither one of us spoke another word as we walked out of the club.

* * *

"Open those mothafuckin' legs and show me that wet ass pussy." I licked my lips.

My dick was hard as a brick watching Morgan lay on top of my red piano with her legs spread open, dipping her fingers in and out of her leaking pussy hole. A nigga was ready to release nut down her throat. Roughly gripping her hair, I slipped my tongue in her mouth and slowly trailed her naked body with kisses. I admired her swollen clit before latching on. Her body squirmed as soft moans escaped her mouth. She was definitely a freak, so I stuck my index finger in her asshole and she moaned even more.

"Fuck! Play with my ass. I love that, daddy," she moaned.

My beard was soaked in her juices and I covered her mouth with mine. I separated our lips before dropping my pants down to my ankles. Lust took over Morgan's eyes as a smirk emerged on her lips seeing my dick standing at attention. Like the freak she was, she got down to her knees, twirled her long ass tongue around the tip of my head, and took inch by inch in her mouth until I couldn't see my whole dick. My tip was slamming against the back of her wet throat as she bobbed her head back and forth. Spit was flying all around her mouth. Her head game was fire, but I wanted some of that pussy.

She gripped the edges of my piano and I sank my dick into her, doggystyle. With every stroke, her phat ass butt cheeks smacked against my pelvis. I was making waves on that ass. We were drunk out of our minds that we didn't stop fuckin' until the next morning and passed out in my bedroom. When the sunlight shined through my bedroom window, I sat up on my bed with the right side of my head pounding while Morgan was slipping on her dress. She rolled her eyes at me before picking up her underwear and putting it in her purse.

"Damn, it's like that? I gave you the best dick of your life," I chuckled.

"How you figure that, fool?" Morgan seemed regretful.

"You kept telling me with every stroke I gave you." I smirked.

"Whatever, clown. Tell anyone and I will deny it. Thanks for the dick, nigga." She gave me the middle finger and strutted out my bedroom with her heels in her hand.

That was a classic freak move.

When I heard the door slam, I climbed out my bed, took a shower, and got ready to go to the cemetery so I could put flowers and balloons on my daughter's grave for her birthday.

Chapter Sixteen
MORGAN REID

Three weeks later...

Ain't no way my old ass was pregnant at forty fuckin' years old from a one night stand. That son of a bitch pull-out game was weak. I angrily snatched some medical papers from the nurse's hand, shoved them into my purse, and stormed out the examination room with my heels loudly clicking on the floor.

Climbing in my car, slamming the door, tears sprung from my eyes as I held my stomach and bent forward, slightly sobbing. A few people who were going inside the doctor's building glanced at me with concern, but kept it moving. I managed to get my emotions under control, taking a deep breath. After wiping my face, I made my way to Maino's house, driving through every red light in the city. When I saw his shiny BMW SUV sitting in his driveway, I pulled my small lock blade pocketknife from my purse before stepping out the car to fuck shit up. Flaring my nostrils, I forcefully stabbed each of his tires watching them deflate. Then I grabbed a crowbar that was in my trunk and shattered his windows, sounding the alarm. A shirtless Maino ran out his front door and approached me with his teeth baring. I began wielding the crowbar at him, making him jump back. An assault charge wasn't a good look for an attorney, but I didn't give a shit.

"What the fuck is wrong with you? Chill the fuck out, Morgan!" he yelled angrily while looking at his shattered windows.

"Nigga, you got me pregnant. Your pull-out game is weak!" I yelled, swinging the crowbar at his bumper, putting a big ass dent in it.

"Pregnant?" his eyes widened.

"Fool, did I stutter? You had one job, and that was to get the pussy and pull out. News flash. You failed, mothafucka," I was angry.

"How do I even know you're pregnant by me?"

Even though I was a sexually fluent woman who loved the company of a man, I knew who the fuck got me pregnant. It was his punk ass. I hysterically laughed at his foolishness before dropping the crowbar and taking off my heel, tossing it in his direction and hitting him.

"Do you think out of all the men in the world that I would blame a baby on you? Hell no." I was blunt.

Maino raked his gigantic hand down his face and sighed, "Let's talk."

Reluctantly, I followed Maino inside his house and he escorted me to the living room. He motioned for me to sit on the couch, but I stood with my arms folded, tapping my feet.

"Sit your stubborn ass down, Morgan. I'll be right back," he told me and left.

"Yeah, whatever. Don't take all day!" I yelled behind him.

I glanced around the living room, and there were photos hanging on the wall along with a beautiful mural of a young girl wearing angel wings. The person who painted it, did a wonderful job. As I ran my fingers over it, Maino walked in holding a bottle of water and a Gatorade.

"That's my daughter Mira." His eyes became glossy as he handed me the bottle of water.

"Wow, she's beautiful," I complimented.

When we were talking, a little girl with curly black hair bolted in the living room holding a baby doll. She leaped in his arms and began playfully pulling his beard.

"Daddy, we got to finish playing dolls," she pouted.

She was the spitting image of her father. They had the same exact caramel skin tone, naturally arched eyebrows, and full lips.

"Give me one-minute, Nova. I have to speak to my friend, Ms. Morgan," he spoke gently.

That mothafucka didn't need to lie to that baby; we weren't cool. He signaled for me to give him a second and scooped her in his tattooed covered arms. He needed to stop stalling. All I wanted to do was tell him that I planned on getting a damn abortion. As I waited impatiently huffing loudly, I heard a door slam and a woman walked in the living room carrying a tiny dog.

"Who the fuck are you? And what are you doing in my man's house?" she looked me up and down with her lips curved in disgust.

"Calm down, baby girl. It ain't that deep," I matched her energy.

"Maino, who the fuck is this bitch? You better come get her before I beat her ass!" she yelled and placed the dog on the floor.

There were a lot of things I didn't tolerate, and disrespect was one of them. I leaped up off that couch so fast and gripped that heffa by her faux locs, damn near pulling them from her scalp. Maino rushed in, wrapping his arms around my waist, trying to pull me off the bitch.

"Stop it, Morgan! You're pregnant."

Maino was trying to break up the fight. Then the dog sank his teeth into his calf, so he had to grip him by the back of his neck and lift him off the floor. It looked like he was getting ready to fling the dog across the living room, but I wasn't having it. I was an animal lover.

"Hold up. Hold up. You better not toss that doggie, Maino. I'm a PETA advocate," I yelled, still holding that stupid bitch's neck.

"Bring that nigga PETA around, and the only thing he gonna be advocating for is this ass whoopin'," Maino spoke through his gritted teeth.

"PETA is an animal organization, not a man," she laughed.

"Lucky for you, it ain't." he was in his feelings.

"Stop talking to this crazy hoe and get her off me!" his little bitch yelled.

"Morgan, you made your point. Let her go please," he asked politely.

"Nope. I told this heffa I ain't the one to play with, but she wanted to talk slick." I was pissed.

"Morgan please. I don't want my daughter to come out and see her mother getting hemmed up," he pleaded.

I thought it was kind of cute of him.

Reluctantly, I released that bitch from my headlock and walked out the front door. There was no way I was staying at his place to talk with his insecure baby mama around. After I climbed in my car, he rushed out behind me, looking confused. His reaction was valid because I did drop a bomb on him about me being pregnant with his baby.

"Where the hell are you going? We got to talk about this." Maino was anxious.

"I changed my mind. If you want to talk, come to my house tonight." I gave him an ultimatum.

I slipped on my Gucci shades and left. A part of me felt guilty about wanting to get an abortion, but I didn't think I would be a good mother. It was time to get on my knees, pray, and hope for an answer.

As I was on my way home, Lovely called and told me my boss, Mr. Carmichael, left an email stating that he needed to see me in his office. After I removed myself from his son's case, he wasn't pleased with my decision. Our conversation got a little heated, and I stormed out of his office. However, there wasn't anything he could do except deal with it. There was no reason to fire me. It's not like he could, anyway. Soon after our meeting, he took a leave of absence from work. I assumed it was to focus on his son's situation. He was facing some serious charges. It broke my heart to know he killed Maino's innocent daughter.

Unlocking my car door, I arrived at my law firm and grabbed my purse. I caught the elevator to the fifth floor where the big boss's offices were located. The front desk receptionist took me back to Mr. Carmichael's office, except he wasn't there, only two detectives. One I was very familiar with and I immediately rolled my eyes.

"Morgan Reid, it's been a long time." He smirked.

"Not long enough, Detective Briggs. What are you here for?"

"My job. Now have a seat," he pointed to the chair.

I took a seat on the leather chair in front of the desk, crossing my legs. He lustfully raked his eyes down my body before he tossed a file in front of me. There were photos of Maino entering my office from the security cameras.

"Is this man the reason why you couldn't take Carmichael's case?" he accused.

"No, I don't even know this man," I lied.

"That's interesting. One of the security guards, who was bloody after this man attacked him, told us you both were familiar. He recalled him telling you to drop the case." He was trying to intimidate me.

"Do you have any proof? Because it sounds to me, those are accusations and not hard evidence. It's his word against mine." I smirked.

"Tell me this, Ms. Reid. how did he leave you standing, while everyone else was laid out on the floor? Your floor."

"Maybe he isn't a woman beater or emotionally manipulative. I don't know what to tell you. Are we done here? I have somewhere to be." I wasn't scared of no damn detectives.

"Detective Jones, you mind if I speak with Ms. Reid alone?" Detective Briggs wanted some privacy.

His partner looked me up and down with a stone face before handing me his card. When Detective Jones shut the door behind him, Detective Briggs stopped the tough guy act. He pulled his lips into a smile and unfolded his arms. When he tried to give me a hug, I balled up my fists ready to knock him out.

"Morg, it's great to see you. You look really good. The last time we saw each other, we both didn't look ourselves," he sighed.

"You were on coke and I was a stressed-out wife. Why are you back in DC? Last I heard, you transferred to Vegas." I was pissed off.

"I'm back; healthy, and ready to get my wife. You know I still love you," he confessed.

"Ex-wife," I corrected him.

Shannon and I were married for twelve years. We were high school sweethearts who tied the knot after accepting our diplomas. While I attended Howard, he went to Bowie State. We lived in a little studio apartment. I was madly in love with him. He couldn't do any wrong in my eyes. I stayed by his side through the cheating and even after he got hooked on pills because of a leg injury that ruined his college football career. My final straw was when he owed money to a drug dealer for some coke, and he came looking for Shannon to kill him. The man beat and raped me. I never told anybody what happened and vowed never to love a man more than I loved myself. We had been divorced for years, so I damn sure wouldn't take him back. There was no love in my heart for him, only malice.

"Look, Morg. Your boss's son is missing, and they believe it connects to the young girl he killed. We can't prove it, but we damn sure are going to find out. Stay safe. If you hear anything, give me a call." He pulled out a card, and I turned my back while frowning my face.

Detective Briggs nodded his head with a smirk and placed it on the desk.

I waited until they left the office. My heels loudly clicked as I walked through the parking garage to my car. I repeatedly hit the steering wheel and then dropped my head, releasing an uncontrollable sob. I managed to get myself together and drove back to Maino's house. His baby mama's car was no longer in front of his house. I angrily banged on the door, breaking a nail. Pain shot through my body as I bit down on my teeth. When Maino opened the door, he was wearing a ripped-up tank top and had scratches on his neck. He allowed me to come in, and there was glass broken on the floor and it reeked of bleach. I found me a seat and glanced around the fucked-up living room.

"What the hell happened here?" I observed.

"You're pregnant and my daughter's mother snapped because of it." He shook his head.

"Don't tell me she did all this because of little ol' me? Maybe if she didn't pop up, her feelings wouldn't have gotten hurt. I am pregnant. What does that got to do with her? Not a damn thing because y'all ain't together. She needs to know her position as the baby mother." I pursed my lips.

"You're in the same position. You're gonna be my baby mother too." He shot me a grin.

"Negro, please. I will never be your baby mother. If I keep our child, I will be your child's mother. And if I wanted to be your wife, I could be that too."

"Yeah, aight. What are you doing back here? I thought I was coming to your place later on tonight?"

"Two detectives came to my law firm and wanted to know why I didn't take the Carmichael case," I sighed.

"For what? That ain't none of their business."

"It is when the client I was supposed to represent, goes missing. It doesn't do any justice when the victim's father, you, storms in my office and beats up security. Did you have anything to do with that disappearance?"

"Don't ask questions you don't want the answer to."

"I'm asking, so that means I want the answer." I was adamant.

"Just leave it alone, Morgan, and worry about having a healthy pregnancy."

"Excuse me? I never said I was keeping this baby." I looked at him like he was crazy.

I pursed my lips as Maino walked up to me and unexpectedly placed his gigantic hand on my flat stomach. My heart rate increased while my breathing intensified. He then dropped to his knees looking up at me with his hooded eyes before kissing my stomach.

"You ain't got no choice, Ms. Reid." He kissed my lips.

Chapter Seventeen
WINTER PRATT

*P*regnant! Pregnant! Pregnant! I couldn't believe that son of a bitch got that loud hoodrat pregnant. My scalp was on fire from that crazy banshee pulling on my faux locs. I had the right mind to press charges and put her ass in jail for assault. There were always some basic tricks trying me because they wanted to be the main woman in Maino's life. They needed to realize they were only being used for their wet asses. I was the wifey and the love of his life. Period!

As I walked through the salon with my purse hiked on my shoulder and rocking a big ass bald spot, my stylist, Courtney, spit out his drink. He then placed his hand against his chest, mumbling to himself before examining the damage to my hair. I just hoped his twenty years of experience would be able to help me.

"Bitch! You look tore the fuck up. What happened to you?" he frowned.

"Girl, my girl cousin did my braids too tight," I lied.

"See, I told you about going to those young hoes. You always want to complain about my prices and look at you now. You comin' up in here lookin' like a bald ass scallywag. You're lucky my man is your cousin because I damn sure wouldn't put you back in my chair. Sit back and let me try to fix this mess. My man will be here soon to take me to lunch." He popped his lips.

"In your car and with your money?" I laughed.

"True, but at least I still got all my hair. Looking like a bald-headed cabbage," he clowned me again.

I rolled my eyes upwards and kissed my teeth. Courtney was a bomb stylist, but he made me sick with his flamboyant ass because he had a smart mouth. That was the main reason why I stopped letting him do my hair. Money wasn't the issue, because baby, I was rich. Being the baby mama to a wealthy kingpin, came with a lot of perks. I never had to look at prices and stayed with my black card on hand. When I got pregnant with our daughter, Nova, from our drunken one-night stand, I secured the bag for a lifetime.

I laid back in the sink bowl and closed my eyes. The cool water felt so good against my scalp. Courtney finished shampooing my hair, and I went to sit in his stylist chair. He poured me a glass of champagne. I gulped it down without enjoying the taste. While he worked his magic on my head, I had several more glasses. I wanted to get buzzed so I wouldn't have to think about my heartbreak. Most people would say I was dumb to stay with a serial cheater, but deep down in my heart, I knew Maino was a good man. In his defense, he told me he didn't want a relationship.

"What's the real reason why you got this bald spot? This look like someone snatched your hair out. Did your baby daddy get a little rough with you? Ain't no man worth getting your ass whipped for." He seemed worried.

"Fuck no! He's a lot of things but a woman beater ain't one of them," I angrily spoke through my teeth with my veins poking out the side of my neck.

I'll admit Maino might've been loose with his dick and made me look stupid in these streets because of the flock of women he had on his roster. However, he never put his hands on me. Even when I became upset and would attack him, he didn't get physical. Occasionally, he tried to retrain me from attacking him, but I could tell, even that made him uncomfortable. After I learned about that woman being pregnant, I bleached all of his clothes, stabbed up his furniture, and fought him. Yet, he remained calm.

"Oh, so which one of his hoes beat your ass?" he snickered.

"First of all, nobody beat my ass, and none of them ever will. I told you my cousin braided my hair too tight." I bit down on my teeth, trying to suppress my anger.

"Ummhumm, if you say so, Winter." He popped his gums.

I tuned that petty bitch out and began flipping through a magazine. My time at the salon flew and my hair was done by noon. Holding the mirror, I smiled looking at my new pixie haircut. Courtney did great hiding my bald spot. I dug in my wallet and handed him some loose cash before slipping on my gigantic shades. With my nose hiked in the air like the bad bitch I was, I strutted out the salon door as those hating hoes looked me up and down with envy.

I climbed in my Jaguar and drove to Tysons Corner Mall for some retail therapy. The display of expensive handbags immediately put a smile on my lips. Sipping on my glass of wine, I began pointing to each bag that I wanted to purchase, as the sales associate eagerly collected them with a smile. Then, I handed the woman my black card and waited for my items to be boxed. She was going to get a huge commission. As I sat down on the luxury furniture, my phone began ringing. I took out my purse and saw it was my father calling me on FaceTime. I slipped on my Airpods and answered. The moment his face emerged on the screen; I could see his long vein pulsating in the center of his forehead. *Why the hell did he look upset?*

"Hi, dad." I smiled.

"What the hell did you do now, Winter?" his jaws twitched.

"I didn't do anything," I was confused.

"I got a call from Maino and he isn't pleased with you. He told me you were acting crazy again."

"Since he likes running his got damn mouth, did he tell you that he got another woman pregnant?" my voice cracked.

"Yes, and he made it perfectly clear, it's none of your business or mine. I agree with him. You and him are not a couple." He frowned.

Of course, my father would agree with Maino because he was a cheater too. He slept around on my mother so much he had her mentally messed up and she committed suicide. She wasn't buried a month before he moved in his long-term mistress, Amy, in our home. She immediately began trying to erase my mother by removing her pictures off the walls and redecorating everything. That made me rageful. When I was fourteen, Amy took a nasty fall while she was two weeks pregnant. She died from blunt force trauma to the head. The coroner, who examined her body, said the cause of death was accidental, but I knew the truth. I killed her ass. I crept behind her as she was walking and shoved that slut down a flight of steps. She never saw it coming, and that made it even more exciting.

"Really, dad? You're going to allow this man to cheat on me." I felt betrayed.

"No, little girl. You allowed it. Maino told you from the beginning, that he didn't want a relationship, but you were persistent. You thought you would be able to change him. He gave you the only man he knew how to be. I'm not going to allow your little heartbreak to mess up business. I make a lot of money. Get it together and stop making trouble. You need to learn how to act like a kept woman. They don't make noise and enjoy the lifestyle that comes with it."

"Maino was right. He is running the show and you're his little bitch. Another thing, you better watch how you talk to me. I'm not the one to be played with. You better hope I can fix this with Maino or you are gonna be sorry," I threatened.

"Take your medication, Winter. You're not acting like yourself and it's not a good look," he grunted.

I screamed loudly with my hands on top of my head, breaking down sobbing. People in the store began looking at me like I was crazy. I didn't care about their stares. My heart was in pain. I looked up to see the sales associates cautiously approaching me, holding out my black card.

"This card keeps declining. Do you have another one, ma'am?"

"This is a new card. Try it again." I squeezed my fists together.

"I did, several times. I need another card, or I will have to put everything back on display. Now, do you have another one or not, ma'am? I have other customers waiting to be serviced." She put her hands on her lower back, hiking her nose at me.

A sinister smirk appeared on my lips as I backhanded the sales associate in the face, causing everyone in the store to loudly gasp. With widened eyes, the red face woman held her cheek in shock before rushing over to the phone. She was probably calling 911, but I didn't give a shit. I actually waited with my legs crossed to see if the police would arrive to arrest me. When two officers showed up, I placed my hands behind my back where they escorted me to their patrol car. I ducked my head down and sat in the back laughing. The female officer turned around to look at me and shook her head, scowling.

"There is nothing funny about going to jail and assaulting an innocent woman. Now stop all that!" she yelled and pointed her finger.

"Please, my dad is Commissioner Pratt, and my Godfather is the Director of the Federal Bureau. I will be out before I get processed. Now shut up. And you better not try any funny business. My life matters."

I winked at both of the white officers and resumed laughing. It felt great smacking that woman, but I couldn't wait to do worse to that bitch who was pregnant by my baby daddy. She was going to regret the day she stepped in our relationship. I was gonna get rid of her and that bastard baby too.

Chapter Eighteen
MAURICE "MAINO" PIERCE

*I*t didn't matter the time or day; I was going to take a drink. Alcohol had become my way to cope after I lost my baby girl. Sprawled out on my king-sized bed with a hangover, the back of my head was pounding, and I could barely keep my eyes open until Morgan walked into my bedroom wearing a silk gown. She began loudly banging on a pot with a gigantic metal spoon marching around, singing off-key. I leaped up scowling, looking at the alarm clock. Her ass was tripping.

"What the hell are you making all this noise for, Morg? It's too damn early for this shit!" I yelled with my hands on my aching head.

"It's three o' clock in the afternoon. You would know that if you weren't up drinking all night. I am not having a baby by a wino. Maybe you need to go to AA to get you some help. I understand you're hurting, but this isn't a healthy way to deal with it."

"Go ahead. I ain't got a problem. I can take a drink, especially when I pay for that shit. Can I do that in peace?" I raked my hand down my face and sighed.

"Oh really? I got something for you." She gave me a dirty look and fixed the bonnet on her head.

With Morgan's nose hiked in the air, she marched out the door. I slowly paced behind her with my basketball shorts sagging off my ass showing my boxers. She began grabbing my expensive liquor bottles from my bar and pouring them down the sink. She ain't have no right to touch shit she didn't pay for in my house. As I reached for the last bottle she was about to dispose of, she shot me a death stare with her perfect beautiful lips pursed up.

"You can drink if you want, but you can't have it in the house. I don't want drinking by our baby."

"The baby isn't even born yet." I raised my hands, confused, and she rolled her eyes.

"Little Milo or Kennedy is in my belly." She touched her stomach.

At first, Morgan was having a hard time accepting the pregnancy, but she was really excited. She started buying books and classical music to prepare. Becoming a father again at my age wasn't ideal, but I was gonna take care of my seed no matter how old I got. Financially and emotionally, I would do my part as a man.

"Who the fuck is that?" I chuckled.

"The names of our kids. I like those the best."

"I ain't naming my son Milo. That's a bitch ass name."

"Why not? It's your middle name? Maurice Milo Pierce," she laughed.

The only reason why Morgan knew my middle name was because her crazy ass did a background check on me. She said she needed to know who her baby daddy was and had to make sure I wasn't no undercover freak. I still had no clue how she managed to get my social security number. Shit like that I didn't keep in house. My job was risky, so I kept it in a vault.

"Exactly, that's why I don't use it. My white ass mother was tripping." I scratched my beard and chuckled.

"Your mother was white? Got damn it, I knew it. That explains why your brother acts like Carlton from 'The Fresh Prince.' God rest his soul." She put her head up to the sky with her hands together.

"Leave my brother out of this and stop messing with my bar. That shit wasn't cheap. All of it was top shelf. Some of those bottles were also imported."

"I don't give a damn. You got a drinking problem, and I refuse to stand here and watch you drink yourself into a coma." She was concerned.

"I told you I ain't got no problem. The only problem I have is you keep telling me I got one. My daughter died. If I want to have a drink, so I don't think about it, I will."

"Well, do what you want, nigga." She angrily stomped off and slammed the bathroom door.

I didn't have time to deal with Morgan and her dramatic antics. Money needed to be made. When I got to my chop shop, stacks of money and bricks of snow were sitting on pallets wrapped up in black plastic. Walking around, I nodded my head with approval before handing one of my truck drivers, Wallace, a duffle bag full of money. He dapped me up and climbed back into his red rig. I pressed a button to open the gate so he could slowly pull out of the loading dock. Immediately, my workers began picking up the pallets using forklifts to take them in a vault that was hidden behind heavy duty shelves. Once everything was stored away, Rich strolled in looking like he needed to get something off his chest.

"Man, what's wrong with you?"

"Remember that bitch, Bailey I fucked a few months ago? The stripper I met at the club?"

"The bitch with the big ass titties who had the homegirl with that phat ass who I took home? Yeah, I remember. That was a good night," I reminisced.

"She's pregnant, and the baby is mine. I got one of those stomach tests." He raked his hands down his face.

"Congratulations, bro. Fatherhood is a good thing." I tried dapping him up, but he ended up looking at me like I was crazy.

"Fuck that, man. I don't want no kids with a stripper. Damn, what am I gonna tell mom dukes? I knew I should have taken my ass home that night, but naw, you was talkin' 'bout turnin' up with the bitches. Now I'm a be financing some stripper bitch's lifestyle."

"You don't have an obligation to take care of her, only your little shorty."

"You right," he agreed, "Aye, you talk to Layla?"

I had been calling my baby mama, but she wasn't answering any of my calls. A part of me felt like she blamed me for Mira's death since I was the one who bought her a car. Eventually, we needed to talk because she was always going to be my family regardless if our daughter was no longer alive.

"I plan to pop up at her place."

"A few days ago, I saw her at some bar, and she was drunk out of her ass. She didn't even look like herself."

"If you see her out again, hit me up."

"No doubt," Rich assured me.

Rich and I dapped each other up before we walked out the chop shop to get into our separate vehicles. Traffic was actually light, so it didn't take me long to get to my house. As I got ready to pull the door handle to step out my truck, my phone began vibrating in my pocket. It was J-Rock calling from prison. We hadn't spoken since we had the disagreement, but he did reach out by letter to send his condolences about me losing my daughter. Even though we weren't on speaking terms, I respected him for still trying to make sure I was straight. If he was ready to chill the fuck out and let me lead, I didn't have a problem with working things out, business-wise.

"Yo, what's good," I answered.

"It's been a minute, Maino. How you been, nigga?" J-Rock probed.

"I'm trying to keep my head above water. You know that's all I can do."

I already knew J-Rock was calling because he didn't have any product left to sell in prison to the inmates. My drug mule had stopped going to sneak him supply after our fallout. I was the boss, and that nigga was gonna learn quickly not to fuck with me. He wasn't gonna eat if he bit the hand that fed him.

"Listen, man. I am dry out here. You know I am always hungry."

"I thought you were going to visit Mexico when you got released. It seems like you had sights on something better." I was referring to him wanting to work with his cellmates' brother.

"DC is my home. I never will betray that. Sometimes things look better, but it ain't. I'm man enough to admit that."

"Glad you see it that way. Tonya told me she is gonna come visit you next week. I'll let you know if anything changes."

"Preciate it, bro. Thanks for not cutting mom dukes off when we weren't in a good place."

"Your mom is good people, and besides, I am a man of my word and always look out, J-Rock." I ended the call.

I slipped my phone back in my pocket and climbed out my truck before heading in my house. Walking into my bedroom yawning, I saw Morgan rocking back and forth with her arms tightly encircled around her body, sobbing. I kicked off my shoes before sitting on the edge of my king-sized bed. Then, I pulled her into my chest and kissed the center of her forehead. She looked up at me with teardrops on her cheeks. I didn't like seeing her upset.

"Why are you in here crying like somebody died, Morg?"

"Why would God make someone like me a mother? I don't deserve this honor. The baby is gonna be speaking ghettonese before she or he knows how to read." She placed the back of her hand on her head dramatically.

"Morg, relax before you give yourself a panic attack. Everything is gonna be fine. You're gonna give birth to a healthy baby. We are gonna raise our child together. You're going to be an amazing mother." I caressed the bottom of her chin.

"How do you expect me to be a good mother when my mother and grandmother used to beat the shit out of me? That's all I have ever known, and I feel like I am bound to do the same thing to my own."

I had experienced the same abuse too. Growing up, my mom would beat the shit out my brother and I for just breathing. Still, her mistreatment didn't stop me from being a good dad. If anything, it made me a better one.

"There isn't a handbook to parenting. You're gonna doubt yourself more times than you can count. But the moment you hold our baby in your arms, all those fears will go out the window. Your sole purpose is gonna be to give them the best life you didn't have. I know you can do this mothering thing, Morg. I believe in you tremendously."

"You do?" she sounded surprised.

"I do, Morg. You're beautiful, educated, funny, and a good friend. I am honored for you to carry our baby."

"I have to tell you something, but you got to promise not to judge me."

"With all the skeletons in my closet, I am the last person to judge. What's up?"

She sighed as more tears began rolling down her face. I immediately sat up to pull her in my arms as she sobbed. Snot was everywhere, but I didn't care. She needed my comfort.

"I had an abortion. It was the hardest shit I had to do in my life, but I couldn't keep a baby that was conceived from rape."

"Rape? Who the fuck hurt you?"

"I don't know his name, but I damn sure would know his face. His actions almost destroyed my life."

"I'm sorry, Morg. That man was a coward."

"Yeah, he was, but it ain't all his fault. My ex-husband gave him the ammunition when he didn't pay his debts. I should've left him a long time ago before it got to that point. Never in my life will I ever give a man that control again. Not even you."

"I understand, baby." I kissed her forehead.

My heart was heavy after Morgan dropped that bomb on me about getting raped and conceiving a child. It really fucked my head up because I knew her ex-husband. He was a corrupt detective that used to work for us. I didn't trust him, so he mainly dealt with J-Rock. There wasn't any point to mention that he used to work for me to Morgan because they were no longer married.

"I don't feel like being in the house. I would like to go get some fresh air to clear my mind."

"Let's go out to dinner to celebrate our baby."

"That would be nice. I want to go somewhere fancy." She kissed my lips.

"I got the perfect place," I wiped her tears. "Thank you for trusting me enough to tell me what you been through. I am gonna try to get better with my drinking."

We got dressed, and I had my driver take us to a spot downtown where they had some good steaks. Opening the restaurant door, Morgan walked in front of me switching those thick hips. I licked my lips, admiring every curve in the red dress she wore. When we approached the brown hostess's booth, some white chick with bleach blond hair looked at us up and down before plastering a fake smile on her face.

"Hi. We would like a table for two," Morgan spoke politely, smiling.

"Do you have reservations?" the host looked down at her computer.

"No, but we don't have a problem waiting until one becomes available."

"Oh, that's unfortunate. We are actually booked up for the evening. Sorry." She smiled.

"No worries. Thank you." Morgan grabbed my hand to leave.

A couple who happened to be white approached the booth. The host greeted them with a chipper demeanor while smiling and even sat them down without a reservation. I peeped the elderly man slip her a bill as she walked to their table. When that bitch returned, I placed my knuckles on the booth and leaned in her personal space as Morgan tried to grip my arm. I wasn't gonna fuck the lady up, but she was gonna learn to know I wasn't the nigga to fuck with.

"I need to speak with your owner." I was sick of dealing with her racist ass.

"Excuse me? She isn't available at the moment. I can take your name and number. She can give you a call."

"That won't be necessary. I will call her myself." I pulled out my phone and the hostess's eyes widened as her face turned ghost white.

The owner, Margie, came out to the front smiling and pulled me into a hug. We met five years ago before her restaurant got popular. I became a silent partner in her business. She immediately escorted us to a private dining room. The chef was told to make anything we wanted, even if it wasn't on the menu. Morgan had a craving for lobster bisque and blackened salmon with char-grilled asparagus and some rosemary potatoes. I ordered me a Wagyu Ribeye Steak. Our plates were placed in front us, and I could see the steam coming off the food. When I grabbed my fork and knife to cut my tender piece of meat, Morgan smacked my hand.

"We got to say grace. You need to be thankful for the food and give thanks to God and the hands that prepared it."

"My baby." I lowered my head, and she grabbed my hand to pray.

We enjoyed dinner, talked a lot, and shared a lot of laughs. Our date night was going great until Ace unexpectedly strolled up to our table with his hands inside of his slack pockets, looking between us curiously. When Morgan began anxiously looking over her shoulders, and tried to duck under the table, I shook my head. I assumed she was trying to hide from Eva. Scowling, I pulled her up from the floor and held her close to me. However, she nudged me away like she was ashamed.

"Ace, what are you doing here? I know what it looks like, but um, we are not on a date. Is Eva here?" she looked worried.

"No, I'm here with my other pops. I saw y'all two when I was going to the bathroom. You two on a date?" Ace probed with a smirk.

That's when a flustered Morgan rushed out the dining hall with her heels loudly clicking on the floor. Her sudden departure had Ace looking at me curiously, but I just shrugged my shoulders and sat back down in my seat. After placing a few bills on the table, I picked up the Cîroc bottle and poured me some more to drink. I couldn't believe she played me in front of my son.

"How long have y'all been fooling around?" I looked at Ace, and he had a goofy grin on his face.

I opened my mouth to answer when Morgan strutted back in our direction, looking sheepish. She came to stand next to me and placed her manicured hand on my shoulders before leaning down to kiss my lips. I assumed it was her way of apologizing for leaving me hanging. It was all good though; she was still my lady. If she wasn't ready to tell everyone we were dating, I was going to respect it.

"Ace, your father is my man. I don't need you telling Eva until I am ready. You know the history between these two, and it's not good," Morgan explained as she looked at me.

"Listen, I don't care if y'all messing around. You both are grown. I just don't want either one of y'all acting crazy if this doesn't work out, but I hope it does. It's a good look for both of you," Ace complimented. "Make sure you tell your friend. I don't want to be in the doghouse if she finds out I knew first. Aight, I gotta bounce."

Morgan and I headed home after she apologized for acting like a coward. The moment I opened the door, she pounced on me. She began pulling off my shirt while kissing on my lips. Picking her up from the floor, she wrapped her legs around my waist, and we began kissing before going to my bedroom. Pussy ain't never been addictive, but I couldn't get enough of Morgan's wetness. She was on her back with her ass hanging off the edge of my bed as I held her legs in the air and pounded away at her contracting pussy. When I slipped her big toe into my mouth, she bit the edge of her lips, making even more sex faces. She was so fuckin' beautiful with her hair wildly on top of her head. I pulled out my dick that was coated in her juices and gently flipped her onto her stomach. Kissing the side of her neck, I slid in her from behind, giving her long steady strokes. Her body began shaking under mine, and I could feel the walls of her pussy squeezing my dick.

"Good girl. Take all of this dick, baby," I sucked on her ear.

"Fuck! Your dick is in my stomach. It's too big," she whined.

"You're always talking about you need a big dick. Now you got one. Push that ass up and take this mothafucka." I fucked her harder.

My nuts were beginning to feel heavy, and I was ready to bust. Nonetheless, I wanted to ensure she climaxed several times before I finally released. Before, I only worried about me getting my nut off while a woman's purpose was to solely be my sexual object. Not when it came to Morgan. I no longer desired to be a selfish lover. I wanted to be the pleaser. I gripped her waist and sped up my strokes. My legs began shaking before I shot my load in her pussy. Then, I turned on my back, and Morgan laid her head on my chest.

We planned to spend the rest of the night chilling, but Morgan passed out sleep while holding her little belly. I didn't want to wake her up with the television and went downstairs to chill for a bit. As I was flicking through the channels laid up on the couch, my doorbell rang. Looking at the golden clock on the wall, I saw it was after nine. I bit down on my lip with anger thinking it was Winter. Snatching the door open, I saw two detectives holding their badges. I was very familiar with one of them.

"Maurice Pierce. The man who killed your daughter is missing, and we have reason to believe you know something about it or had something to do with it. You can either come down for questioning voluntarily, or we can get a warrant for your arrest and come back. But if we come back, we will not be this calm. We will get a warrant to search this entire property," the white detective said.

"I ain't got shit to hide like your partner Shannon."

"It's Detective Briggs. We are not playing. You can come with us and answer questions now or we come back later in a different fashion, and you answer the questions. However, you will answer for this." Shannon mugged me down.

"I'll be down there in an hour." I slammed the door in their faces.

I knew it was a matter of time that the detectives would try to bring me in for questioning for the Carmichael disappearance, but they weren't going to find anything. I made sure of that. I quickly got dressed and did my best not to wake Morgan up. On my drive to the precinct, I hit up my attorney and told him what was transpiring.

I sat inside the semi-lit interrogation room smirking at Shannon, who kept his head down to the floor like a bitch, as his fat ass white partner called himself questioning me. He was slamming his fist on the table and getting in my personal space to intimidate me. My jaws flexed, and I was ready to break his jaw. Yet, holding my composure was needed unless I wanted to catch an assault charge for beating a detective's ass. All I did was shrug my shoulders and ignore the questions. I paid my lawyer to speak for me. When he got there, he would handle the rest.

"You have a motive, Mr. Pierce. This man killed your daughter and you're telling me you didn't want revenge? I think you did. Why did you do it? You realize Chase Carmichael's father had money and pull. You assumed you wasn't going to get justice and took matters into your own hands?"

"Back up out my mothafuckin' face. I ain't under arrest," I grunted and slammed my hand on the desk.

"Watch your tone with me, boy," Detective Jones sized me up.

"Naw, you better watch how the fuck you talkin' to me."

"What you gonna do about it? You plan to make me disappear?" Detective Jones said.

A slight chuckle escaped from my lips. I didn't respond because that fat mothafucka was trying to bait me. There was a knock on the door and my attorney, Penson, barged his way in the room before setting his sights on the detectives.

"My client will no longer answer any questions. He is dealing with the death of his daughter from a heinous accident, and you have the nerve to treat him like a suspect."

Shannon wanted to act tough with my attorney, "He has a motive. That's why we brought his ass down here for questioning."

"My client wasn't even in the states when Chase Carmichael was reported missing. He was with his family in Maui, mourning the death of his precision daughter. So, if there's nothing else, my client and I will be leaving. If you continue to harass him, we will have your badges."

My attorney pulled out a vanilla folder and slammed it on the table. I already knew what was in there—my alibi. There were copies of my flight records to Maui, phone records showing my location, and printouts of my credit card statements. Ace made sure he used my phone several times and went to many stores to purchase items with my black card to make it look like I never left Maui.

"If you were a better husband than you are a detective, I wouldn't have your woman. I'll make sure not to drop the ball and keep Morg safe," I whispered to Shannon.

"You mothafucka." Shannon called himself running up on me, and his partner grabbed him.

I stood up from the chair with a smirk on my face and strolled out the doors of the precinct. Leaping in my truck, I started up the engine as Detective Shannon Briggs stood outside scowling. If he tried to get in my way, I was going to put that nigga in the dirt where he belonged.

Chapter Nineteen
MORGAN REID

Loud banging and shouting could be heard coming from the front door as I sat with my feet up biting into an apple. It was probably Maino because he didn't even know that I got my cousin who worked as a locksmith to change the locks to his own house. I refused to let him back in, not until we came to an understanding about respect. He would not sneak out after giving me some bomb dick and lay up with another woman especially when I was pregnant. Hell, to the naw. When my cellphone began ringing, a huge grin spread across my face seeing his number pop up on my screen.

"Hello, Big Maino." I bit back my smile.

"What the fuck going on? My keys ain't working."

"Yeah, I know. I got the locks changed."

"You did what? That's my damn house you in. I didn't tell you to do that. Stop playin', Morg and let me in my house." He was angry.

"Not until you tell me where the hell you have been? You think you're gonna just be slinging your big dick across town and leaving me here barefoot and pregnant? Fuck no. I don't know what type of weak women you're used to dealing, but that ain't me. I am nobody's jump-offs. Either we are together or not. I don't have time for the games."

"C'mon, Morg. You're paranoid. What makes you think I was with another woman? If you open the door, I can explain where I went. Please."

Maino was looking like a sad puppy through the peephole, so I let him in. With a smirk, I stepped to the side as he strolled in the foyer of the house. He immediately pulled off his sweat hood and tossed it on the floor. That's when I picked it up to follow him upstairs where he went into the master bathroom to take a shower. I sat on the bed waiting for him to hear what he had to say. When he entered back in the bedroom with a towel around his waist and water dripping off his body, I bit my lip.

"Put your clothes on. Don't think that you are going to distract me into some erotic shit. I need to know what made you sneak out." I folded my arms against my chest.

"Two detectives showed up here and wanted to question me about Chase Carmichael's disappearance. They didn't even have a warrant, but I knew they would be back, so I followed them down to the precinct."

"Oh my goodness. Without your attorney present? Are you crazy? They are gonna put your black ass in prison, and I'm going to be a single mom. Lord, help. What are we going to do? Should we go on the run? You got a lot of money and we can start a new life."

"We ain't going on no run. I ain't been in this game all these years to be taken out by some pigs. Those mothafuckas ain't got nothing on me, Morg. My alibi is straight, and my attorney gave them information that proves I was in Maui when that Carmichael dude disappeared. Now stop stressing out my baby." He rubbed my stomach.

"Good. I really didn't want to have to go on the run with a baby in me, and I am not raising our baby by myself. Matter fact, when was the last time you saw your youngest daughter?"

"It's been a minute. I am just trying to get my mind right," his voice cracked.

"Oh, hell to the naw. You need to pick her up and spend time with her. I understand you're in a lot of pain dealing with the loss of Mira, but your parenting obligations doesn't stop for Ace or Nova. I refuse to let you be a deadbeat on my watch."

"You're right, baby. I am going to handle my business. Thank you for keeping it real."

"Always, baby. Now your key is in your sock drawer. Don't make me take it back. I don't care about you paying the bills. Anyway, can you take me to get my fur baby? I miss him."

"You want him to come to my place?" he raked his hand down his face looking stressed.

"Yes, I miss my fur baby." I smiled.

"Ummmm, aight," he reluctantly agreed.

I stood on my tippy toes and slowly kissed his lips. He got dressed before grabbing his car keys and drove me to get my fur baby. As I sat in the passenger seat, he kept his hand protectively on my belly. When we arrived at my condo, I eagerly put my unit code in and busted through my front door. Maino slowly walked behind me, looking around all paranoid. Searching around my living room, I found Tink, sleeping in his plush multi-cat tree condo. I snatched him up with a smile and snuggled my baby close to my body as Maino grimaced. After nuzzling my nose against Tink while he loudly purred, I placed him on the floor, and he arched his back in the air with his claws out.

Poor Maino stepped back towards the door with his eyes popping out his head like he was scared of cats. He was too funny. He was gonna have to get used to my fur baby because he was my loyal companion. Grappling two plastic bags, I packed up Tink's litter box, gourmet fancy cat food, some soft toys, and bowls before we left. On the way back to Maino's place, we stopped at 7-11 so I get my snukkums a few Fiji water bottles. Maino turned off his engine and looked at me cradling Tink, who was sleep and wrapped up in a blanket. Tink would get skittish and cry hysterically if I put him in the kennel, so I held him to give him comfort.

"What do you need for me to get for you? You know you can't be eating all that junk food. It ain't good for the baby." Maino was concerned.

"I don't need any of that. Just get a few Fiji waters. I plan to go to the store soon. Fruit is really good for the baby."

"Oh, you like that fancy shit, huh? You don't like my Deer Park? That explains why I still got a lot in the refrigerator."

"I grew up in Baltimore drinking tap water. I will drink anything, but my Tink only drinks Fiji."

"Get the hell out of here? You about to make me go in here to get some Fiji water for this bougie ass cat," he ranted and opened the car door to go inside the store.

A few minutes later, Maino strolled out holding three bags and placed them in the backseat. We quickly drove back to his place. The moment we got into the house, Tink began meowing loudly before running behind one of Maino's couches. Tink was very hesitant and shaky because he was in an unfamiliar spot. Maino headed to bed, and I walked my fur baby around the property to familiarize him with the new environment. My eyes were becoming heavy, so Tink and I went upstairs to the bedroom. I smiled seeing Maino knocked out with his hand over his head, loudly snoring. When I climbed under the covers holding my cat, Maino wrapped his arms around us. That's when he leaped up looking crazy with his bug eyes. He zoomed in on Tink like he was about to snap. His jaws were twitching.

"What the fuck, Morg? I ain't sleeping with this cat. Get this furry nigga out my bed!" Maino shouted.

"Oh no. I can't let Tink sleep alone. We have been sleeping together since I got him from the shelter. This is my baby."

"No, that's the baby," Maino pointed at my belly, "This furball belongs on the floor," he was adamant.

"Well, since you don't like pussy cats on your bed, I ain't giving you no more of mine that's between my legs. How about that?"

"You gonna do me dirty like that, for this dirty, furry ass animal? Man, shit... I'll let him stay here, but make sure his fishy breath smelling ass stays close to the edge by you or I am booting him."

"Aww, Tink. Your daddy didn't mean it. Don't worry, you're going to grow on him." I patted Tink as he purred.

A smile emerged on my lips as Tink laid at the bottom of my feet and went to sleep. He seemed to be a little more comfortable, so I was able to close my eyes resting against Maino's bare chest. Maino thought about me not giving him any pussy. He was right to change his mind about my Tink. My fur baby wasn't going anywhere. We were a package deal.

I woke up to in the morning to the smell of bacon and eggs. With my bonnet still on my head, I snatched it off before freshening up. I walked down the stairs and stepped on a damn Lego. Pain shot through my body as I bit down on my teeth, ready to yell and curse, until a smiling face little girl approached me holding a ball. It was Nova. She didn't say a word but grabbed my hand like she knew me for years and led me to the kitchen where Maino was standing over a hot stove flipping bacon on a cast-iron skillet.

"Nova, didn't daddy tell you Ms. Morgan was sleeping? My bad if she woke you." He grabbed the last few pieces of bacon and put them on a plate.

"No, daddy. I didn't wake her up. I was being a good girl." She was so innocent.

"Yes, you were, honey. Leave this baby alone. What you need to focus on is not burning up the bacon. Where is my fur baby Tink?"

The sound of meowing caught my attention, and I followed it to the laundry room. Opening the door, I saw my fur baby Tink walking around meowing loudly. I picked up my baby before marching towards Maino to give him a piece of my mind.

"Oh, man. There you go Tink. I was looking for you, little homie." Maino was full of shit.

Maino tried to act like I ain't know he locked Tink up in the laundry room.

"Silly daddy. You asked me to put him in there," Nova giggled.

Maino shot me a sheepish grin and kissed my cheek. Then, he put a plate of food on the table for me. The kicker was when he poured Tink some Fiji water like they were cool. He was just trying to stay on my good side for locking my fur baby in the laundry room. I sat down at the table to eat. When the three of us were done breakfast, I left them alone so they could bond. As I walked past the playroom, my stomach dropped listening to Nova ask her daddy when her sister was coming home from heaven. I couldn't imagine how they were feeling as a family.

Sticking my head through the crack of the door, I watched as she sat on Maino's lap while he read her a children's story. It was about a loved one who passed away. Holding back my tears with my lips quivering, I softly shut the door and went to find a comfortable outfit for my lunch date with Eva. We weren't spending a lot of time together because of the many changes in our lives, so I always looked forward to bonding with her. After I put on a nice shirt, jeans, and some black Nikes, I grabbed my tote bag. Maino walked me to my car, giving me a hot kiss before watching me pull off.

I met Eva at some restaurant downtown. She was already sitting at the table holding my god baby. I sat down, placing my purse in the chair next to me, and picked up a menu. The waiter came to bring us some lemon water before giving us a few minutes to order. A smile emerged on my face seeing Eva's interaction with her daughter. She was an amazing mother. I was hoping to be one too.

"Hey, chica and little chica." I gave them air kisses.

"Look at you glowing, boo. Life is still treating you great. How have you been?" Eva handed me my god baby.

"Fabulous. What about you? How are you juggling motherhood, being a wife, and working as that bomb professor? I swear it's been forever since I saw you."

"I love it. At first, I thought it was too much to handle, but I figured out it's all about prioritizing. And when I really think about it, I am living out a lot of my dreams." Eva beamed.

"So happy for you, boo. How is Ace?"

"He's fine. He supposed to go hang out with Maino today." She rolled her eyes.

"Why you roll your eyes? I thought you and Maino would be cool by now. He is your father-in-law," I joked, and Eva sighed.

"I am never going to be cool with that thug. The only reason why I tolerate him is because of Ace and my princess." She was transparent.

"Maybe he changed. I think you should give him a chance and get to know him." I was pushing my luck.

"The hell if I will deal with him. Remember that thug almost got us kicked out of school. And he still in the streets selling that shit, I bet. Let's not forget how much of a dog he is."

"True," I sighed.

***

Sourness overtook my throat as I rushed to the bathroom in my office and planted my head into the toilet to vomit. My sleeveless dress suit was going to get ruined sitting on the floor. I felt terrible and couldn't keep any food down. Already the baby was giving me a run for my money. My doctor gave me some medicine to help, but the shit wasn't working. After I was done, I rinsed my mouth out and tossed a little water on my face. Sighing, I walked out to grab my briefcase to go home. As I was walking through the hallway, I heard a few whispers from my colleagues. They had been acting strange towards me, but I figured it was because our boss had those detectives talk to me. He hadn't returned back to the office since his son went missing. A part of me felt bad because I knew he would never see his child alive again, but the other side of me, felt like he got what he deserved for taking an innocent life—my man's daughter. I pressed the button to get on the elevator as my colleague, Sandy, bumped into me. That bitch chose the wrong day to be clumsy.

"What's your damn problem? You can't see or something," I looked at that bitch with my jaws locked.

"That you're still working here when you have something to do with my boyfriend missing. I saw the tape. You know that man. He is the girl's father who Chad accidentally killed."

When she tried to swing on me, I tossed my briefcase on the floor and got ready to scrap. However, I refrained from doing so because of the growing life that was in my belly. I had to start thinking about the safety of my unborn child. One of the men from the office grabbed her back and scooped her over his shoulder as she called me all types of bitches. That heffa even had the nerve to spit in my direction. I tightly squeezed my fists together, taking deep breaths. The Lord knew I wanted to cave her whole face in. She was lucky that I was pregnant, and security was called because it was almost a fight. The security guard kept pressuring me to answer questions like a cop and shit. I refused and tossed the pen along with the piece of paper when they wanted me to write a statement. I knew my rights. They weren't even cops. That crazy woman attacked me, so I had grounds to sue. I stormed out, mumbling under my breath and got on the elevator.

My adrenaline was still pumping as I climbed in my truck. When I got to Maino's place, tightness took over my chest. A detective's car was sitting in front of his house. I knew who was in that car, and I was fuming inside. I marched up to the window and started banging. Shannon rolled it down, smirking. As for his partner, he reached for his gun.

"Just like a trigger-happy white fuck. You gonna shoot me? Matter fact, I wouldn't be surprised if you did anyway. Y'all be shooting us down like animals... But let me remind you primitive thinking brutes that I am human just like you. I hope you understand that simple concept of life, but if you don't, forget you."

"Calm down, Morgan. He is just having a bad day. Put that shit away," he firmly ordered his white partner.

I could tell his white ass had a problem listening to a black man tell him what to do.

"What the hell are you doing here?" I probed.

I needed to be careful of my words because they were most likely surveilling Maino to build a case. However, I knew they didn't have anything on him. They were gonna try everything in their power to find some dirt. If they couldn't get him for the disappearance of Chase Carmichael, they would try to take down his drug empire.

"We have reason to believe the man who lives in this house sells drugs," he revealed.

"What man?" I knew Shannon was on some bullshit.

"Maino, the man you told me you didn't know, but that is a lie because you're at his house. Let me guess, you're fuckin' him, and that's why you didn't take the Carmichael's case," he spoke through his gritted teeth.

I opened my mouth to speak as Maino strolled out the house wearing a white tee and jogger sweatpants, looking good. He immediately approached the car with his muscles flexing. I could tell from the pulsating vein on the side of his head that he wasn't in the mood. Protectively, he pulled me close to his chest and kept his hand on the arch of my back as Shannon burned a hole through his head.

"What seems to be the reason why y'all are outside of my property, detectives?" Maino spoke through his gritted teeth.

"We are detectives. And detecting shit." Shannon frowned and squeezed his steering wheel.

"I don't care who the fuck y'all are, nigga. Get away from my property or I will have your badges."

"You ain't going to do shit. We are the law." The white detective mugged Maino down with strife.

"I am above the law." Maino smirked arrogantly, and we strolled back to his place before slamming the door.

We didn't bring up the fact that my ex-husband and his partner were sitting outside his house. However, I could tell it bothered Maino regardless of how calm he tried to act in their presence. Deep down he knew they were going to try to find any evidence to get him off the streets even if it meant intimidating people to get them to testify about his drug operation. In my line of work, I saw it too many times. That made me slightly nervous because my job and law license were in jeopardy if I refused to cooperate. Nonetheless, I would never rat him out to the FED's and would take his confession about killing Chase Carmichael to my grave.

"Do you think he will be a problem? He now knows I am your lady. I suspect he will try to make your life a living hell because of it."

"Fuck that chump nigga. He ain't running shit but his mouth. I'm about to go holla at Rich for a minute. I will bring back dinner so you ain't got to cook."

He cupped the side of my chin and kissed me long. Whenever his lips connected to mine, I lost my train of thought. I watched him strut out the door with his back muscles flexing and smiled. Then I went to take a bubble bath before climbing in the bed. My fur baby, Tink, laid curled up next to my body until I drifted off to sleep.

***

I was sick and tired of my husband, Shannon, not answering his damn phone. His ass always claimed to be working so he didn't have time to answer. However, that's a damn lie because whenever I called his job, he was never there. Even though he was a detective who worked long hours, I knew he was on some bullshit. Slamming down the house phone, I marched to our bedroom. With tears easing down my cheeks, I began snatching his expensive suits off hangers and other clothes before shoving them into duffle bags. That nigga could go be with that bitch who he was fucking. It was time for me to free myself. As much as I loved Shannon, I was tired of putting all the effort into saving a marriage that was broken. When I looked in the mirror, I didn't recognize myself. I was losing weight and my hair was falling out from stress. After I packed all of his shit, I went to sit it outside the front door of our apartment just as a brown skinned man wearing a trench coat approached me. He had a distinguished slash under his right eye. When he licked his lips, I could feel the hairs all over my body raise up.

"How are you queen? Is Shannon here?" he rubbed his chin.

"He no longer lives here. Have a good day," I walked off.

When I went to shut the door, he put his big dress shoe in between the door and the entrance. Then he forcefully pushed it back hitting me dead in the face knocking me on the floor. I immediately started seeing stars and felt my face swelling up. Panic took over my body as I watched him close the door and put the lock on it.

"What do you want? Please leave," I was scared.

"Your husband owes me a lot of money. Now he is dodging my calls, so I figure since I can't get it back from him, your pussy will be a better payment," he licked his lips and reached for his buckle.

"Somebody help me!" I screamed.

My pleads for help were silenced when he took out a gun and pointed it at my head. The sinister smirk he had on his face made my stomach drop. When he began walking over to me with the gun still trained on me, I continued to sob. He towered over my shaking body and had the audacity to call me a beautiful woman. When he moved a piece of my fallen hair out my face, I hawk spat on his face. Rage brewed in his eyes as he smacked me with the butt of his gun. He pulled down my pants and climbed on top of me. I did my best to fight him off and kept trying to close my legs. However, he was too strong. He pinned my arms above my head and roughly stuck his dick in me. His hot breath lingered on my neck. Through my loud sobs, I heard him grunting as he sped up his strokes. My pussy was on fire and it felt like he was ripping me open. Several more times he *pumped into me while he roughly kissed my lips before cumming inside me. Then, he zipped up his pants and left me a bloody mess on the floor.*

God knows how long I stayed there sobbing, but when I stood up, there was an excruciating pain between my legs. I picked up the phone to call the police but then slammed it down deciding against it. I was an attorney and knew how the system worked. It would be months before he could be prosecuted. I didn't have the mental stability to stand trial or testify.

As I walked outside my apartment ready to get in my car to end my life by running into a lamp post, a tiny kitten was sitting under my car. When the kitten approached my feet meowing, I scooped the animal in my arms and held it close to my chest. It was like God put the kitten there to save me.

I popped up from my sleep sweating and saw Maino sitting on a chair next to the bed. He didn't utter a word. He just looked at me with those piercing hooded eyes like he was worried. That's when he stripped off his clothes and climbed onto the bed. I shifted more in his direction as he slowly kissed my neck.

"Are you okay? You kept screaming for help."

"I am fine baby. Just had a bad dream."

"About what?"

"Nothing."

"Whatever you need Morg. I am here for you. You do know that, right? I care about you a lot."

"I know you're here for me. Thank you, baby," I kissed his lips as Tink came to snuggle next to me.

"You really love that nasty cat don't you?"

"Yes, I do because Tink saved my life," tears sprung from my eyes.

As Maino held me close to his beating chest, I cried my eyes out. I truly believed that the right man had finally came into my life. A man who could truly love and protect me.

Chapter Twenty
JARELL "J-ROCK" GIBSON

*P*rison wasn't for the weak. There was always some mothafucka testing your gangster and trying to make a name for themselves behind them walls. I only had a day before my release day, so you know a nigga was trying to keep his hands clean. About ten years ago, a cop named Nathaniel Brooks, that used to be on my payroll, planted drugs at my mansion and arrested me because his fiancée accused me of raping her. Truth be told, I had raped a few bitches that were frontin' on me, but deep down, I knew shorty wanted a nigga. That hoe had been trying to throw her pussy at me for the longest time. She used to wear tight outfits knowing a nigga was gonna look whenever I was around. I unexpectedly popped up at her place one day. She assumed I was there to visit her man to discuss business and let me in. Sometimes men let their temptations get the best of them, and that's what happened to me. I ended up taking that hoe's pussy. The end result led me to lose my freedom and the keys to the empire that I reigned over.

The yard was crowded with inmates and CO's, watching us like hawks. I laid back on the bench press and gripped the barbell. Rep after rep, I had sweat dripping off my face. You had to show your strength and earn your stripes in the yard so mothafuckas didn't think you were weak. My cellmate, Javier, approached me with some other Mexican dude, who had devil horn tattoos on his forehead.

"What's good, homie? Did you speak to your boy on the outside? My brother is ready to make a move." Javier sounded like he was ready to do business.

"Yea, I finally spoke to him. His daughter died so he's been in a bad spot," I explained. "He heard about the product y'all was selling to your clients. People been dying left and right, and that ain't good for business if you got bad product. You want mothafuckas to get high, not die. Most importantly, he ain't trying to get cased up by the feds fucking with y'all, but give me a little more time so I can talk some sense into his head. My word is bond."

"Orale, I trust you, Rock. Let me just speak with my brother and see if he can wait a little bit longer. I'm telling you, holmes, we trying to make some boss moves," he dapped me up. "What if he ain't down with the move?" he probed.

"He ain't going no choice. My hard work built that organization, and he is going to get in or be put down," I gritted.

"I thought that was your homie from way back?"

"Ain't no homies in the drug game, only business." I rubbed my chin.

The prison siren sounded off, letting us know it was time to go back inside for lunch. I hated being told what to do by those mothafuckin' pigs. A nigga couldn't wait to be released. I followed the rest of the inmates as the CO's did their best to contain order. It was always risky between transitions. You never knew what a mothafucka was ready to do. Men amongst men, egos were like ticking time bombs. They could go off any second, whether that be one inmate shankin' another over some beef, or simply to let mothafuckas know they ain't the ones to be fucked with. A lot of them were doing life in prison and would never be free, so taking a person's life didn't faze them. I walked into the chow hall with the other inmates and got in line to be served. My stomach began to turn sour looking at the food. I wouldn't feed that shit to my dog... but hey... a nigga had to eat to survive. Then, some big, black, bald headed nigga with a lazy eye just had to buss in front of me and take the last roll that was meant for me. He proceeded to skip the line like no one was going to check him.

"Hey man, don't you see we all in line?" I sized him up.

"Yea, but I don't give a fuck, nigga. What you gonna do about it, you pretty ass nigga?" he blew a kiss at me.

Word around the prison was that dude liked to take niggas asses. He was an ass bandit. Bearing my teeth, I walked up to him and knocked his tray out of his hands. I didn't give a shit that he towered over me scowling and flexing. Bitch ass nigga. He wasn't gonna treat me like some faggot. As I was about to attach my fist to that mothafucka's jaw, a male CO rushed in between us to defuse the situation. I put up my hands and stepped back, while Big Blackie kept talkin' shit. He was lucky. I ended up settling for a hard ass grilled cheese sandwich, and the damn cheese wasn't even melted. Meanwhile, the mothafucka who took the last roll kept provoking me. I just shook my head and kept eating, though.

A CO named Watkins, approached my table and said someone was there to see me. Something wasn't right because visiting hours were over, but I tossed my food in the trash and got escorted to an unfamiliar room. A confused expression appeared on my face seeing Detective Shannon Briggs sitting at a table wearing a gray suit. He used to be on my payroll, but I let him go because he had a bad ass coke habit. He went from me giving him money to keep the feds at bay, to getting in debt with me. That was bad for business. I sat across from him and began massaging my beard.

"What are you doing here, Detective?" I folded my arms and mugged him down.

"I came here to see an old friend. I heard you're getting out tomorrow. Congrats," he was sarcastic.

"Nigga., you ten years too late. I been here. Now cut the bullshit. What you really want?" he had the worst bluff.

"I want Maino."

"For what?"

"Murder. I believe he killed the drunk driver who killed his daughter. I need you to get him to confess to it on tape."

"Get tha fuck outta here! I ain't a rat!" spit flew out my mouth.

"I figured you would say that, Rock, but if you help me get Maino off the streets, you will be back on top. You already know I am willing to keep the law off your ass. I got a few more officers who would be down to work too. You and I both know you can't play number two."

I calmly chuckled, "For a mothafucka who carry a shield, you are sure are the dirtiest of them all. You supposed to be good; a hero of the community. To serve and protect. Me, I don't have that problem. I live up to my dirt. My job is dirty and I'm a dirty, ruthless mothafucka. I ain't know your wife had some good ass pussy until you let me rape her to clear your debt." I smirked.

"Don't bring Morg up." Detective Briggs' jaws locked.

"I wish I could remember how she looked like. Y'all still together?" I probed.

Detective Shannon didn't respond. He just slipped me his business card before he got up from the table and left. I got escorted back to my cell. While I laid back on my bed looking at the ceiling thinking about how I could set Maino up, the sounds of keys jingling caught my attention, and my cell door opened. A CO named Bridget came in on me holding her handcuffs. We immediately locked eyes before she strutted in my direction with lust dancing in her hazel eyes. I had been slinging my dick to her for years. She turned a blind eye to all the illegal shit and stayed putting commissary on my books. With a smirk on my lips, I put my hands behind my back before she gently placed them on my wrist. She then gripped my arm and escorted me to the shower room. It was lockdown time. All inmates were supposed to be in their cells sleep and shutting the fuck up.

Dropping my jumpsuit, I bent her ass over as she laid her hands against the tiled shower walls. I sank into her from behind and her mouth formed an "o." When she began pushing back, I sped up my strokes. It didn't take me long to shoot my load inside of her wet ass pussy. After wiping the sweat beads off my head, I pulled my pants back up and waited for her to get dressed so she could take me back to my cell. It was always a wham-bam situation with her, but she looked like she was stalling. She pulled out a sonogram from her uniform, and I felt a tightness in my chest. I didn't want any kids. My legacy was supposed to die with me.

My jaws locked and my nostrils flared, as I gripped hold of her neck up against the wall with her feet dangling off the floor. Her face began to turn blue and I released my grip. She dropped on the floor and I towered over her. She had me amped enough to start kicking her in the stomach. Her sobs were beginning to grow, so I pressed my hand against her mouth. Panic appeared on her face because she didn't know if her life was going to end.

"You tricked me, bitch. It's taking everything in my power not to snap your neck. If you have this baby, I ain't helping you raise it. Scandalous ass bitch," I gritted.

"How can you talk to me like that? I have done everything for you; even left my husband. You talk to me this way? Like I am nobody? It's because you're leaving, right?" she sobbed.

"At the time you were something to do. Now I don't need your fat, black ugly ass. My time here is done and so is this situation. Now take me back to my cell." I put my hands behind my back.

She wiped the tears with the back of her hand and took me back to my cell. I wasn't worried about her snitching on me because she knew her job would be on the line. Since she was going to be a single mother, she needed all of her income. With my hands behind my head, I shut my eyes and fell asleep.

The next morning, I walked out the prison gates a free man and saw Maino leaning up against his truck. He pulled me into a dap before we climbed into his ride back around the way. Before starting up the engine, he handed me a bottle, and I popped it open, spilling some of the champagne.

"Welcome home." Maino nodded.

"Nigga, it's good to be home." I smirked.

I took the bottle to the head and laid-back, thinking about moves to take Maino down. There wasn't no such thing as loyalty in the drug game. I knew that when I killed my own pops to take his throne.

"What you trying to get into tonight?" Maino probed.

"I am trying to get up in some pussy. Where the bitches at?"

"Tomorrow, we are having a welcome home party for ya at the club. But today, my girl is gonna cook for you. We can just chill at my spot."

"A nigga ain't have a home cooked meal in ten years. You know I'm down."

"Let's go to your new place so you can get dressed. Check the glove compartment. I got you a new phone there and a couple stacks to hold you over until you get a job."

"'Preciate you looking out." I grabbed the latest iPhone and stacks.

We blasted the music, and I bobbed my head. Maino took me to my new condo downtown. DC had sure changed since I had been locked down. There was a bunch of white people walking around carefree with their dogs. My spot was already decked out with furniture, and my refrigerator was stocked. I changed into some new fresh gear and then we headed to his place so his woman could cook.

Maino lived in Potomac, MD in those big houses. I climbed out of his truck before following him inside. The smell of spices engulfed my nostrils as we entered his foyer that had a big ass crystal chandelier above. Maino escorted me to his living room, and I plopped down on his couch.

"Get comfortable, nigga. Grab the remote and turn on the sports," he said and left.

After turning on the television, I took out my new cellphone and began texting my girl, Andrea. We had been together before I got cased up. As I raised my head up from the screen, a beautiful woman with some thick hips and a fat ass entered holding a bottle of champagne and two glasses. She was a baddie. I would fuck her.

Her eyes widened when she saw me and dropped everything on the floor. I got up to help her, but she jumped back with panic etched on her face. When Maino came back, she damn near knocked him out the way running out the room.

"Everything good in here?" Maino looked at me and then the broken bottle and glass cups.

"Your girl dropped the bottle. She got startled when she saw me. My bad."

"You good. Let me get this glass up."

Maino swept the glass up and grabbed another bottle. He handed it to me, and I took it straight to the head to celebrate.

"When we gonna get to work? I am trying to stack this paper." I placed the bottle on the coffee table.

"I will set a meeting with you with a new crew. They will report to you," Maino told me and I nodded.

Picking back up the bottle, I placed it against my lips when Maino's girl came in holding a gun, shaking with tears rolling down her cheeks. She pointed the gun at me, and my eyes widened.

"What are you doing with my gun, baby? Put that away," Maino pleaded.

"No, this is the mothafucka who raped me because Shannon owed him money. He is gonna pay for what he did," she sobbed as she closed her eyes and pulled the trigger.

I leaped up from the couch, getting grazed in the shoulder, as she kept on shooting in my direction. Bullets were flying, and I quickly ran past Maino to get out the way. He was struck twice before dropping to the floor in a pool of blood. I didn't have time to worry about that nigga when his crazy bitch was trying to kill me. When I reached the foyer and opened the front door, I heard a gut-wrenching scream.

"Oh, my goodness, Maino! I didn't mean to hurt you! I love you!" that chick screamed.

To be continued...

CONNECT WITH ME

Kendra Necole, a Washington, D.C. native, and a lover of words, started her journey reading and majoring in Education. Making a difference in children's lives is something that is near and dear to Kendra's heart. She believes every child deserves the right to quality education, no matter of their social or economic status in the world.

Escaping deep within the pages her favorite fiction novels is how Kendra balance her home, work, and schooling schedule. And in addition to her love of reading and educating, writing has always been an escape as well. Finally mastering the demands of what a successful path should look like, Kendra took to putting her all into writing. Once she realized her dreams didn't have to be limited by boxes and parameters other set, Kendra buckled down and penned her first novel in the Urban Romance genre. Releasing Twisted Off That Cali Love in 2020, Kendra was immediately able to see the fruits of her labor. Her first novel topped number one on the Amazon charts, and she followed that release up with five additional books within the span of a year and a half.

Knowing that she doesn't have to choose one path to walk, Kendra now focuses on her career as an Author, all while continuing to stay dedicated to her passion as an Educator. Kendra embodies, hard work, loving life, and remaining true to herself.

Facebook: https://m.facebook.com/kendra.canty.7
Instagram: www.instagram.com/authorkendranecole

Made in the USA
Las Vegas, NV
07 April 2025